Girls Go Home!

Lindsay jogged across the lawn to Founder's Hall, and then paused at the front steps to slip her map and schedule inside her notebook. Suddenly, she heard a soft whooshing sound above her head. She looked up just in time to see a big red balloon plummeting down at her.

With a shriek, Lindsay threw herself onto the grass. The balloon hit the sidewalk right next to her and burst with a loud *splat!* Cold water flew up and drenched her face, hair, and blouse.

"Girls go home!" a boy's voice called from somewhere over her head. "We don't want you here!"

BOYS' SCHOOL
Girls

RANDY'S RAIDERS

by Francess Lantz

Rainbow Bridge®
Troll Associates

For Susan,
     thank you for your idea and your generosity.

and

For Elvia,
     who helped me put the words in Elizabeth's mouth.

CHAPTER ONE

*L*indsay Tavish stood outside the door of the Randall Hall School auditorium and swallowed hard. Her stomach was doing back flips and a tropical storm was brewing in her armpits.

"Good morning, boys," said a deep, rumbling voice from inside the auditorium. "Welcome to the first day of school."

Lindsay couldn't see the owner of the voice, but she knew it belonged to the school's headmaster, Mr. Bertozzi. Closing her eyes, she tried to imagine the scene inside the auditorium.

She pictured Mr. Bertozzi, with his thinning brown hair and pale, squinty eyes, standing behind a podium at the front of the stage, addressing the all-male student body. In Lindsay's anxious imagination, the auditorium was the size of the Rose Bowl, and every square inch of space was filled with boys. Hundreds of boys, thousands of boys, millions of boys, boys as far as the eye could see . . .

Mr. Bertozzi's voice brought Lindsay back to reality. "Most of you probably know by now that this year marks the beginning of a new era at Randall Hall School for Boys—I mean, Randall Hall School," he was saying. "At the end of last year, the trustees voted to admit girls to the school for the very first time."

Lindsay heard the boys whispering among themselves. There was laughter, a couple of whistles, and a chorus of loud boos.

Lindsay resisted the urge to peek around the half-opened door. Instead, she glanced at the three girls who were standing in the hallway with her. One of them, a pretty girl with huge eyes and thick, wavy brown hair—Marissa, Lindsay thought her name was—was biting her fingernails. Another, a tall blond girl with dangling fish earrings—Angora or Aurora, something like that—was bouncing from foot to foot. The third, a short girl with straight black hair and restless dark eyes—Lindsay couldn't remember her name at all—was staring at the floor.

"Sounds like they're forming a lynching party in there," Lindsay said with a nervous laugh.

The girl with the fish earrings let out a loud burp. "I think I'm going to hurl my breakfast," she announced.

The pretty girl ignored her. "Does my hair look okay?" she asked no one in particular. Before Lindsay could answer, the girl bent over at the waist and furiously began fluffing up her curls with her fingers.

Through it all the girl with the straight black hair kept her eyes glued to the floor.

Lindsay's heart sank. Here she was about to face her first day as one of only four girls in an all-boys' school, and her only allies were a space cadet, an aspiring supermodel, and a zombie.

Inside the auditorium, Mr. Bertozzi clapped his hands. "Boys!" he said in a booming voice. "Silence!"

The whispering and booing stopped.

"Now, without further ado," Mr. Bertozzi announced, "I want you to welcome the four girls who will be joining this year's sixth-grade class. Girls, come in, please."

Lindsay's heart leaped into her throat. She looked over at the others. They looked back at her, their eyes wide with shared horror, and for the first time since they had all been introduced in Mr. Bertozzi's office a half hour ago, Lindsay felt a real bond with her female classmates. *We're in this together,* she thought. *Just the four of us in a school full of boys. Hundreds of boys, thousands of boys, millions of—*

Suddenly, the girl with the fish earrings leaned over and threw up on Lindsay's shoes.

Lindsay gasped and leaped backward, slamming against the door with her elbow. "*Yow!*" she cried as her funny bone buzzed with pain.

"*Ew!*" the pretty girl shrieked, pointing at the mess on the floor. "Gross!"

"Sorry," Fish Earrings said in a small voice.

The quiet girl reached into her purse and silently handed Lindsay a wad of tissues. Ignoring the vibrating pain in her elbow, Lindsay grabbed them and hurriedly wiped off her shoes.

"Girls," Mr. Bertozzi boomed, "where are you?"

Lindsay tossed the tissues into a nearby wastebasket, straightened her glasses, and whispered, "Here goes nothing." Then she pushed open the door and walked into the auditorium.

The Randall Hall School auditorium turned out to be much smaller than the Rose Bowl. But as Lindsay gazed across the sea of boys in their identical uniforms—navy blue jackets, white shirts, blue and white striped ties—the effect was pretty much the same. There weren't millions of them—only 214 sixth, seventh, and eighth graders—but they were all staring at her. The fact that they were staring at the three girls walking behind her, too, was small consolation.

Lindsay glanced down self-consciously at her clothes. The school didn't have uniforms for girls—not yet, anyway—so Mr. Bertozzi had told them to wear skirts or dresses. In her pink blouse, paisley scarf, and plum-colored skirt, she felt like a peacock in a herd of sheep.

"Hey, Four Eyes," a voice whispered as she walked up the aisle, "why don't you go back where you came from? Randy Hall is for boys only."

"Yeah," another voice chimed in. "Girls stink!"

Lindsay's cheeks were burning, but she fixed a serene expression on her face, lifted her head high, and kept walking. It was a trick she had learned from her family, experts in breaking new ground without breaking a sweat.

Lindsay came from a family of firsts. Her father had been the youngest civil court judge ever appointed in Pennsylvania's history. Her mother was the first woman director of Middleford County Hospital. And her big brother, Fraser, was the only kid ever to win the East Coast Junior Sectional tennis championships without losing a single point.

Lindsay had never been first at anything—until today. With her heart in her throat, she climbed the stairs to the stage and stepped up beside Mr. Bertozzi. Standing beside him was Ms. Iver, the girls' adviser. Lindsay had met her briefly in Mr. Bertozzi's office that morning. She was young and pretty, with curly brown hair and no-nonsense green eyes. She noticed Lindsay looking at her and smiled encouragingly.

Lindsay smiled back, and then turned and looked out across the auditorium. The boys stared back. The only face she recognized belonged to an eighth grader—her brother, Fraser. He caught her eye and stuck out his tongue.

If only Fraser didn't go to Randall Hall, too, she thought for the hundredth time since she had received her acceptance letter. She thought back to what he had told her before they left the house this morning. "I don't want you embarrassing me in front of my friends," he had said. "So try to pretend you're a normal person instead of my sister, okay? And for once in your life, don't say anything stupid."

Lindsay sighed. Why couldn't she be like the rest of her family? They breezed through new situations like hawks with good tail winds, charming everyone in sight even as they were shaking up the status quo.

Lindsay, on the other hand, was famous for speaking her mind, even to the point of alienating everyone around her. Not that she ever meant to upset people. But when she knew she was right, she just had to speak up. It was only later, when her temper had subsided, that she usually found herself wishing she had been a little more tactful and a lot less loud.

Like the time she heard the hostess at a local

hamburger hangout tell a group of black teenagers there were no tables, and then turn around and seat a group of white teens. Lindsay had stood up in the middle of the restaurant and loudly demanded an explanation. Not that it had done any good. The hostess had ignored her, she couldn't prove anything because the black kids had already left, and everyone stared at her as if she had a second nose growing out of the top of her head.

Then there was the time she had written the sentence, "The workmen razed the house down the street," in one of her fifth-grade English papers. Her teacher had told her that the word was spelled *raise*, and that it meant "to lift up" not "tear down." She had borrowed the library dictionary and proven him wrong in front of the entire class, which was probably why he gave her a C- on every English paper she wrote the rest of the year.

Lindsay groaned inwardly. She had an entire mental scrapbook of embarrassing memories like those. Now, as Mr. Bertozzi cleared his throat, she gratefully turned the page on the past and gave him her full attention.

"First of all, boys," he began, "I'd like you to welcome Ms. Iver, the school's first female teacher. Ms. Iver will be teaching English. She will also be the girls' adviser."

Ms. Iver stepped up to the microphone. "Hi, guys," she said. "I know what you're thinking and the answer is no, you will *not* be able to get away with murder in my class just because I'm a woman." She laughed. "Now that we've got that out of the way, I'm sure we'll get along just fine."

Wow, thought Lindsay, *she really told them!* She glanced at Ms. Iver and smiled. Ms. Iver smiled back.

"Well, boys," Mr. Bertozzi continued in a hearty voice, "I'm sure you're all eager to get to know your new classmates. So I'm going to ask each girl to step forward and introduce herself."

"Puh-leeze!" the girl with the fish earrings whispered. "What does he think this is, the Miss America pageant?"

Lindsay giggled. "Maybe I should have worn an evening gown," she whispered back.

"Aurora Barclay," Mr. Bertozzi said loudly, "would you like to go first?"

Aurora gasped and stepped forward. Looking at her, Lindsay was sure no one would ever guess she had thrown up less than five minutes ago. Aurora was the picture of health as she bounced from foot to foot, stopping only to push her sun-streaked blond hair out of her eyes. She was wearing a loose-fitting turquoise cotton dress with a picture of a lizard silk-screened across the front. Crystals dangled from her necklace, and her fish earrings seemed to swim as she moved.

"Tell the school a little bit about yourself," Mr. Bertozzi said encouragingly.

"Well," she began, fingering her necklace, "my name is Aurora and, like, uh, I moved here from California at the beginning of the summer. I'm into surfing, except, well, you know, there isn't any ocean here—except for the Jersey shore, of course, only the waves aren't as big as in Malibu. Anyway, I want to be an actress. Or maybe an astrologer. Or a rock star."

Yikes, Lindsay thought, *what a flake!* Still, Aurora seemed friendly, which was more than she could say about Randall Hall boys so far.

The next girl to step forward was the quiet one who had given Lindsay the tissues. She had waist-length, shiny black hair that was pulled back into a ponytail, and she wore a simple white blouse and a green plaid skirt. Her skin was the color of coffee ice cream, and she had tiny silver earrings in her pierced ears. "I'm Elizabeth Lopez," she said in a haughty voice. "I'm Mexican-American, in case you couldn't tell." She stepped back into line so fast, her ponytail whipped through the air like a black snake.

"What's her problem?" the girl with the big eyes whispered. "I mean, my grandparents come from Italy, but I don't make a big deal out of it."

Lindsay glanced over at Elizabeth. She was staring at the floor again.

"Marissa, would you like to be next?" Mr. Bertozzi asked.

The pretty girl's big eyes got even bigger. She stepped forward and burst into a high-pitched giggle. "Hi," she said in a lilting voice. "I'm Marissa Petrini." Marissa was wearing a red dress with white, lacy leggings. "I like dancing, football games, basketball games, and . . ." She giggled and her brown curls bounced around her cheeks. ". . . football and basketball players."

The boys groaned and rolled their eyes. A few eighth graders whistled. Marissa giggled and stepped back in line.

With a sinking feeling, Lindsay realized she was the only girl left. As Mr. Bertozzi turned to her, she stepped forward and gazed out over the faces of the boys. They stared back at her with expressions ranging from boredom to outright disgust.

Then her eyes landed on Fraser. He was sitting with his best friends, Mason Fitzpatrick and Phillip Mankowitz. Both boys were poking Fraser with their elbows and whispering in his ears. Fraser responded by pushing away their arms and sliding down in his seat.

As Lindsay watched, he looked up and his eyes met hers. She smiled, but he shot her a warning look that seemed to say, "Remember what I told you this morning."

"Lindsay, please go ahead," Mr. Bertozzi said impatiently.

Lindsay's knees began to wobble, and her heart ricocheted against her rib cage. This was it. Her chance to start over. No one at Randall Hall except Fraser had a clue about her alarming tendency to put her foot in her mouth. All she had to do was think charming, think gracious, think *Tavish*.

Lindsay took a deep breath and began to speak.

CHAPTER TWO

*M*y name is Lindsay Tavish," she said in a firm, clear voice. "I'm proud to be one of the first girls at Randall Hall, and I hope someday I can make you proud of me."

"That's easy," a cute, sandy-haired boy in the second row whispered. "Get lost." The boys around him snickered. Mr. Bertozzi shot them a look and they stopped.

"I think opening Randall Hall to girls will bring the school into the 1990s," Lindsay continued, trying to ignore the boy and concentrate on being charming. "Today girls can be anything they want to be," she went on, "doctors, lawyers, astronauts, architects—"

"Or just a goody-goody pain in the butt," the cute boy whispered.

Lindsay looked at the boy's smug face and her temper

rose like a thermometer on a hot day. Suddenly, her mind went as blank as an empty computer screen. When she spoke, her voice seemed to be coming from someone else.

"Oh, yeah?" she cried. "Well, for your information, I am going to be the first woman president of the United States. Top that if you think you can!"

For an instant the room fell silent. Then the entire auditorium burst out laughing.

Oh no! Lindsay thought, her cheeks blazing with embarrassment. *Why didn't I keep my big mouth shut?* It was true, she did dream of being president someday. But it was her secret fantasy, not the kind of thing she went around telling everyone. In fact, until today she had never shared her dream with anyone except her mother and her diary.

"Boys!" Mr. Bertozzi bellowed, clapping his hands. "Silence! *Silence!*"

The laughter slowly died out. Lindsay hoped Mr. Bertozzi would punish the sandy-haired kid for taunting her, but instead the headmaster went on talking as if nothing had happened.

"I'm sure Lindsay's last name rings a bell," he said breezily. "Her brother, Fraser, is the star of the Randall Hall tennis team." Mr. Bertozzi gestured to where Fraser was sitting. "Let's hope Lindsay will be as much of an asset to the school as Fraser is."

Lindsay wanted to dig a hole and crawl inside it. She avoided looking at Fraser. She was certain he wanted to wring her neck.

"Thank you, girls," Mr. Bertozzi said, motioning to four empty seats in the front row. Gratefully, Lindsay and the others sat down. "And now," he continued, "it's time for one of our Randall Hall traditions. For the benefit of all the new sixth-grade students, we always ask one of our eighth graders to talk a little about the history and traditions of Randall Hall."

"Bo-ring!" Lindsay heard a boy behind her mutter.

Mr. Bertozzi didn't seem to notice. "However, this year," he said, "we've decided to choose a sixth grader to speak." He smiled. "I think when I tell you his name, you'll understand why. It's Charles Bennington Randall IV. Chas, will you come up here, please?"

Lindsay looked at the good-looking boy who stood up, and did a double take. It was the kid who had called her a pain in the butt!

He strolled to the front of the auditorium, straightened his tie, and gazed out at the audience with his piercing blue eyes.

"My great-great-grandfather founded Randall Hall in 1902," he began. "Back then it was called Randall Hall Day School. You may be wondering why he opened a middle school instead of an elementary school or a high school."

"Because he didn't have enough money?" Aurora whispered. Lindsay, Marissa, and Elizabeth giggled.

"Charles Randall, Sr., felt that the ages eleven through thirteen were the most important time in a *boy's* life," Chas continued. As he said the word *boy's,* he looked right at the girls.

Lindsay felt her temper heating up again. *What a snob!* she thought.

"My great-great-grandfather wanted to create a place where middle school *boys* could learn and grow," he went on.

Lindsay scowled. Not only was Charles Bennington Randall IV a snob, he was a liar. She sat on her hands and told herself to ignore him, but he was looking straight at her. "Without any unimportant distractions," he added significantly.

Lindsay's hands shot out from under her legs. "But that's not true!" she blurted out.

"Wha—?" Chas gasped.

"Young lady . . ." Mr. Bertozzi began.

"Well, it's not," Lindsay said, rising to her feet. "When I found out I'd been accepted at Randall Hall, I went to the library and read all about Charles Bennington Randall. He never said anything about making this a boys' school. It's just that back in 1902 when the school opened, no girls applied. Then later, after Charles Randall died, the trustees voted to keep the school boys-only."

"Er . . . she's right, you know," said a gray-haired teacher in the back row. "I'm writing a book on the history of the school, and that's the way it happened."

"Way to go, Lindsay!" Aurora said in a loud whisper. Marissa giggled, and even Elizabeth smiled.

"Now, now," Mr. Bertozzi broke in, "let's not argue. What happened in the past is not really important. The fact of the matter is that, starting today, Randall Hall is co-ed. So let's just make the best of it."

Make the best of it? Lindsay thought indignantly. *The way he talks, you'd think the school year was a picnic that just got rained out.*

But before she could decide whether or not to speak up again, Mr. Bertozzi cleared his throat and said, "Thank you, Lindsay, for setting us straight. And, Chas, thank you, too. I think that's enough tradition for one day. You may sit down."

Chas made a face at Lindsay. Then he turned and stomped back to his seat.

A second later the bell rang. The boys jumped up and headed noisily for the door. "Have a good day," Mr. Bertozzi called after them. "Let's make this Randall Hall's best year ever!"

The girls grabbed their notebooks and followed the boys out into the grassy quadrangle that separated the auditorium from the other buildings. Immediately, Marissa selected a cute boy from the crowd and stopped him to ask for directions. Elizabeth hugged her notebook to her chest and took off without a word. That left Lindsay and Aurora.

"You were totally awesome in there," Aurora said, flipping her hair off her shoulders.

"I was?" Lindsay asked doubtfully. "I felt like an idiot."

"No way. Besides, what about me? First I barfed all over your feet, then I got up in front of the boys and babbled like a brain-dead Valley girl!" She fingered her earrings. "Do you have any idea where we're supposed to be now?"

Lindsay smiled. Aurora was definitely a space cadet, she decided, but kind of interesting. She didn't take herself too seriously; and, unlike Lindsay, she didn't seem to worry about doing and saying the right thing all the time.

In fact, talking to Aurora almost made Lindsay stop worrying about Fraser. *After all, what had she done wrong?* she asked herself. Chas Randall had told a lie and she had corrected him, that's all. *Fraser should be proud of me,* she told herself.

With renewed confidence, Lindsay pulled out he schedule and map. "Let's see," she said, "sixth grade, sectior A, first period. Looks like we have to go to Founder's Hall. According to the map, it's that three-story brick building with the green shutters on the other side of the quad."

"Wow, not only do we move from class to class, we even move around from building to building," Aurora remarked. "I don't think we're in elementary school anymore, Toto," she added, imitating Dorothy in *The Wizard of Oz*.

Lindsay laughed. "Follow the yellow brick road," she said as they started down the path. The quad had emptied out except for one or two boys who seemed to know exactly where they were going. They stared suspiciously at the girls as they walked by.

Lindsay ignored them and looked instead at the buildings that lined the quad. Long ago they had all been part of Charles Bennington Randall's estate. The library had once been a carriage house, the auditorium had been a barn, and Founder's Hall had been Mr. Randall's home.

As the girls strolled past the library, Lindsay looked up at the larger-than-life bronze statue of Charles Bennington Randall that stood out front. "Nice place you've got here, Charlie," she said.

Aurora laughed. "It's a lot different from L.A., that's for sure. I mean, I'm used to 'swimmin' pools, movie stars,'" she drawled, quoting "The Beverly Hillbillies" theme song. "Not falling leaves and preppies."

"You actually know movie stars?" Lindsay asked.

Aurora didn't answer. "Hey, is that your brother?" she asked, pointing down the path.

Lindsay looked up to see Fraser walking toward them. She was about to call out to him, but then she hesitated. At home Fraser was just plain old Frase, her big brother. But here at Randall Hall, everything was different. Fraser Tavish was a well-known, popular eighth grader, while Lindsay was just a lowly sixth grader—*and* a girl. Should she talk to him, or should she wait and see if he talked to her first?

The question was answered when Aurora asked, "What's wrong? Why are you stopping?"

Lindsay realized she was standing unmoving in the middle of the sidewalk. Fraser was only ten feet away and getting closer. "Uh, uh . . . hi, Fraser," she finally blurted out.

"Hi," Fraser said, stopping beside them. He wasn't smiling.

"This, uh . . . this is Aurora," she said. "Well, I mean, you know that, don't you?"

"Greetings," Aurora said, bouncing from foot to foot.

"Hi. Lindsay, can I talk to you a minute?"

"Sure, Frase," Lindsay said. "You go ahead," she told Aurora. "I'll catch up with you."

As Aurora walked away, Fraser turned to her. "Lindsay, why did you have to shoot your mouth off in Assembly? Now all the guys are calling you President Lindsay and asking me if they can be your running mate. It's embarrassing."

"I'm sorry," she said. Talking with Aurora, Lindsay had almost managed to convince herself that Fraser wouldn't be mad at her. In fact, deep down she had even hoped he might be a little impressed with her knowledge of school history, not to mention her courage. But now, gazing up into his frowning face, the truth seemed totally obvious, and she felt like a real dweeb.

"Oh, forget it," Fraser said, grabbing her head in the crook of his elbow and giving her a noogie. "Just try not to be so . . . so *Lindsay*. You know what I mean?" With that he turned and walked away.

Sighing unhappily, Lindsay watched him go and then hurried to catch up with Aurora. But her friend was nowhere in sight, and Lindsay decided she must have gone inside Founder's Hall.

Lindsay jogged across the lawn to the building, and then paused at the front steps to slip her map and schedule inside her notebook. Suddenly, she heard a soft whooshing sound above her head. She looked up just in time to see a big red balloon plummeting down at her.

With a shriek, Lindsay threw herself onto the grass. The balloon hit the sidewalk right next to her and burst with a loud *splat!* Cold water flew up and drenched her face, hair, and blouse.

"Girls go home!" a boy's voice called from somewhere over her head. "We don't want you here!"

"Yeah," shouted another voice, "you're all wet!"

Lindsay looked up just in time to see a head covered with thick, sandy-colored hair disappear inside an open third-floor window.

*L*indsay sat up and pushed her damp hair out of her eyes. She gazed down at her blouse. There was a large water stain right over the middle of her chest. *Oh, terrific,* she thought, scrambling to her feet. *This should give the boys plenty to talk about.*

Suddenly, a first-floor window opened and Ms. Iver stuck out her head. "Are you planning on coming inside, Lindsay? Or should I just set up your desk out there?"

"Someone dropped a water balloon on me," Lindsay said indignantly. "Someone named Chas Randall."

Ms. Iver gazed silently at Lindsay for a moment, taking in the scene. Then she said, "Come inside and let's talk."

Lindsay hurried into Ms. Iver's classroom. The rest of the class was already there. Elizabeth was sitting in the back row. She had pushed her desk a few feet away from the other students and was staring at her hands as if they were the most fascinating objects on earth. Marissa, on the other hand, had selected a seat in the middle of the room, surrounded by boys. Aurora was sitting in the front row. She caught Lindsay's eye and mouthed the word "bummer."

Lindsay scanned the boys' faces as she walked to the front of the room. To her surprise, she saw Chas Randall sitting in the third row with a smug smile on his face.

"Class," Ms. Iver said firmly, "I want all of you to write a short essay on the best thing and the worst thing that happened to you over the summer. Now start writing." Then she turned to Lindsay. "Okay, what happened?"

"Chas Randall dropped a water balloon on me from the third floor," Lindsay said.

"That doesn't seem possible," Ms. Iver replied. "Chas was in his seat when the bell rang."

"Well, it was someone with sandy-colored hair. I saw him. Besides, who else would do a dumb thing like that?"

"Lots of boys, I'm afraid," Ms. Iver answered. "Change is a scary thing for some people. And Randall Hall is definitely changing."

"But we're just girls," Lindsay said. "What's so scary about that?"

"Put yourself in their shoes. How would you feel if you went to a school that had always been all-girls and suddenly a bunch of boys showed up?"

"It would be weird," Lindsay admitted. "But I wouldn't try to embarrass them in front of everyone."

Ms. Iver folded her arms and fixed her green eyes on Lindsay. "Speaking of embarrassing someone, you have to admit you came on a little strong in Assembly today. You really stole Chas's thunder. I'll bet that hurt his pride."

"But I was just telling the truth. Besides, he was coming on strong, too—like he owned the school or something."

Ms. Iver smiled. "I'll let you in on a little secret. I guess you know that the school's nickname is Randy Hall, right?"

Lindsay nodded.

"Well, some of the teachers—the ones who knew you'd have trouble being accepted—have been calling you girls Randy's Raiders."

"But we're not—" Lindsay began, but Ms. Iver cut her off.

"You may not think of yourselves as raiders, but in a way, coming into an all-boys' school is a little like launching an attack." She laughed. "And, Lindsay, you hit this school like a linebacker sacking a quarterback."

Lindsay felt her cheeks burning. Things were moving too fast. She had come to Randall Hall eager to fit in and to make her family proud of her. Instead, she'd been here less than an hour and already Fraser was mad at her, Chas Randall hated her, and Ms. Iver had her pegged as some sort of loudmouthed women's libber. "I'm sorry," she said. "I didn't mean to embarrass Chas or make anyone mad. I guess it's like my father says—sometimes I talk first and think later."

Ms. Iver shook her head. "Don't apologize. The things you said in Assembly this morning were one hundred percent right. But here's a word to the wise—until the boys get used to having girls around, it might be better if you tried fitting in instead of sticking out like a sore thumb."

"I'll try," Lindsay said. "I promise."

Ms. Iver sighed. "I'm glad Mr. Bertozzi agreed to put all four of you girls in the same section. You're going to need to stick together and help one another out." She smiled. "Lindsay, why don't you go to the girls' room and see if you can dry off your blouse a little?"

"Okay," Lindsay said gratefully. "Where is it?"

"Uh, come to think of it, there isn't one in this building." Ms. Iver thought for a minute. "There's a boys' room down the hall to the left. Just knock before you open the door."

Lindsay gulped. "But . . . but . . ."

"Go on," Ms. Iver said, giving her a gentle push. "I used it myself earlier. And hurry back. We've got a lot of work to do this period."

Reluctantly, Lindsay stepped out into the hall and closed the door behind her. Then she stopped, gathering up her courage. She'd never been in a boys' room before, although once at the mall the janitors had left the men's room door open while they were cleaning it and Lindsay had sneaked a peek inside.

Lindsay walked down the hall, glancing at the old paintings of Charles Bennington Randall and his ancestors that decorated the walls, and thought about what Ms. Iver had told her. "I'm glad Mr. Bertozzi agreed to put all four of you girls in the same section," she'd said. "You're going to need to stick together and help one another out."

Lindsay frowned. She could imagine being friends— or at least friendly—with Aurora. But she wasn't sure she wanted to "stick together" with Marissa and Elizabeth.

Marissa came off as a boy-crazy flirt, and Elizabeth acted like an untamed pony, ready to bolt at any moment.

The words BOYS' ROOM painted on a heavy wooden door brought Lindsay back to the moment. She inched forward, half-frightened to even touch the doorknob. But she knew that was silly, so she knocked loudly and then leaned her ear again the door. Silence. She knocked again, even louder. Nothing. Finally, she took a deep breath and slowly opened the door.

With her heart drumming against her ribs, Lindsay took a step forward and peered around the edge of the partition. Then she saw him—a boy! He was standing at the sink with the water running full blast.

Lindsay shrieked and leaped backward. At the sound, the boy whipped around, spraying water on the mirror, the paper towel rack, and the floor. When he saw Lindsay, he gasped and jumped back against the sink.

"I . . . I . . ." he stammered. "Aren't you . . . I mean, isn't this . . . I mean—"

"It's my fault," Lindsay said hurriedly. "I thought . . . that is, Ms. Iver said . . . er, uh—"

"Look, I'll leave," the boy said. The water on his hands was dripping onto his pants.

"No, you were here first," Lindsay insisted, backing away.

"No, no, girls before boys," he said.

"No, first come, first serve," Lindsay answered.

"No, no, age before beauty," he shot back.

Lindsay stopped, puzzled. She stared at the boy. He was grinning. Suddenly, they both burst out laughing.

"I'm sorry," Lindsay said between giggles. "Ms. Iver

told me to use this bathroom. I knocked first, but I guess you couldn't hear me."

"It's not your fault," he replied.

For the first time since she encountered the boy, Lindsay took a good look at him. He was about three inches shorter than she was, and thin, with curly brown hair, a turned-up nose, and freckles. His school tie was crooked and his face was smudged with dirt.

"What happened to you?" she asked.

"Chas Randall pushed me into a mud puddle," he admitted. He gazed at the water stain on her blouse. "What about you?"

"Someone dropped a water balloon on my head," she said. "I thought it was Chas, but I guess he has an alibi." She glanced at the boy's hands. "You're dripping."

"Oh!" He grabbed a damp towel and pressed it against the front of his blue pants.

Lindsay felt her ears get hot. "I'll wait outside."

"No, I'm done," the boy said, turning off the water. He looked in the mirror and used the paper towel to wipe away the smudges on his face. "It's all yours," he said as he hurried past Lindsay and walked out the door.

Alone in the bathroom, Lindsay blotted her blouse dry with a paper towel and washed off her shoes with soap and water. Then she combed her hair. On the way out, she glanced at herself in the mirror and smiled. The absolute worst thing had happened—she had met a boy in the bathroom. Yet, amazingly, it had turned out all right.

Lindsay adjusted her pink hair band, flipped her long, brown hair behind her shoulders, and left the room. To her surprise, the boy was waiting for her.

"Just thought I ought to introduce myself," he said with a lopsided smile. "I'm Henry Bartholomew. Sixth grade, section B. And you're Lindsay Tavish, the girl who one-upped Chas Randall."

Lindsay shrugged with embarrassment. "I didn't mean to. I just opened my mouth, and the next thing I knew, my foot was in it."

"Hey, I'm grateful," Henry teased. "Up until today, Chas and his pals have devoted all their time to torturing me. Now that you're on the scene, they'll have someone else to concentrate on."

"I know why Chas doesn't like me," Lindsay said, "but what does he have against you?"

"Chas Randall has been beating me up since we were both in diapers. It started in preschool. He knocked down my blocks, so I called him Skunk Breath. Next thing I knew, I was facedown in the sandbox. It's gone on like that ever since."

Lindsay giggled, but her words were sincere. "Chas sounds like a real bully."

Henry shrugged. "Don't worry about me. I may be small for my age, but I'm fast." He reached into his jacket pocket and took out a quarter. "When Chas gets in my face, I disappear." He waved his fist past Lindsay's ear and then opened his hand. The quarter was gone!

"How did you do that?" Lindsay asked with delight.

"I'm a magic buff. Come on, I'll walk you back to class."

They started down the hall in the direction of Ms. Iver's room. Lindsay's chest felt like a cage filled with excited hummingbirds. She couldn't believe she was actually walking and talking with a boy. Not that she'd never talked with a boy before, but—well, come to think of it, she realized she really hadn't talked with many boys, unless it was about a school assignment or they were friends of her brother or something like that.

"Check out this painting," Henry said, stopping in front of a formal portrait of Charles Bennington Randall. "Notice the low forehead, the glazed eyes. Obviously, old Charlie was a few croutons shy of a salad."

Lindsay giggled. "I guess it must be kind of tough for Chas, being surrounded by so much family history all the time. I mean, everyone expects you to uphold the family tradition and everything." She thought about her own family, and suddenly she felt a little sorry for him.

"Oh, he eats it up," Henry replied. "That's why you girls make him so mad. He's been looking forward to coming to Randall Hall his whole life. But now that he's finally here, everyone is paying more attention to the four of you than to him. It's got to be killing him."

"You don't look too sad about it," Lindsay pointed out.

"After the way he's treated me?" Henry smiled mysteriously and reached into his pocket. "You know what I'd like to do to Charles Bennington Randall IV?" He pulled out his hand and flung something at the floor. There was a loud *pop!* and a puff of white smoke appeared.

Lindsay gasped, and then burst out laughing. "That's amazing!" she exclaimed. "How'd you do it?"

"I told you I was a magician."

"Oh, come on, show me," she urged. "I won't tell anyone. I promise."

Henry considered, and then reached into his pocket and pulled out a marble-sized ball wrapped in pink paper. "Magic fireballs," he explained. "They're made from tiny amounts of explosive chemicals. Toss them against something hard and *kapow!*"

"Where did you get them?"

"You can buy them at magic stores," he said, "but I make my own. My parents are both chemists and they buy me the stuff I need." He grinned. "They call me the mad scientist."

At that moment the door to Ms. Iver's room flew open and Chas Randall appeared. "Lindsay," he said in a singsong voice, "Ms. Iver sent me to look for you. You didn't fall in the toilet or anything, did you?"

Lindsay didn't answer. "You dropped that water balloon on me, didn't you?" she demanded.

"I'll never tell," Chas said with a grin. "But I'll let you in on a little secret. There's an elevator in the back of the building that not many people know about. It can get you from the third floor to the first floor real fast." He wrinkled his nose and sniffed the air. "Hey, what's that smell? It's like smoke or something."

"Probably a short circuit in your brain," Henry quipped. "Faulty wiring, I expect." Lindsay giggled.

Chas shot them both a dirty look. "You think you're pretty smart, don't you? America's first woman president and her trusty sidekick, little Peanut Boy. Well, don't get too comfortable, Tavish. By the time I'm done with you girls, you'll wish you'd never heard of Randall Hall. And as for you, Henry, why don't you make like an egg and beat it?"

"Did you say egg?" Henry asked innocently. He waved

his hand behind Chas's back and produced a plastic egg. "Looks like you laid another one, Randall."

"Come here, you twerp!" Chas growled, lunging for Henry. His hand slapped the egg, knocking it to the floor. It bounced wildly and rolled against the wall.

Chas lunged again, but Henry was ready for him. He ducked, turned, and jogged off down the hall. "Catch you later, Lindsay," he called over his shoulder.

An instant later Ms. Iver stepped into the hall behind Chas. "Is there some problem out here?"

"No, ma'am," Chas said innocently. "Lindsay was just coming back. I was holding the door for her."

Lindsay nodded obediently and hurried into the classroom. But Chas's threatening words were still echoing in her head. *By the time I'm done with you girls, you'll wish you'd never heard of Randall Hall.*

Lindsay took a seat and sighed deeply. The way things were going, she felt as if Chas's threat was already coming true.

CHAPTER FOUR

What happened to you?" Aurora asked, hurrying up to Lindsay as soon as the bell rang. "I mean, you went to the lavatory and didn't come back for fifteen minutes. I thought you'd been assassinated by a squad of guerrilla girl-haters or something."

Lindsay laughed. English class had made her forget her problems, at least temporarily. She loved the way Ms. Iver ran the class—more like a round-table discussion than a lecture—and she was excited about the subjects they were going to be studying. Along with the usual reading and grammar, there was going to be lots of writing, public speaking, and even some debating. *Just the kind of stuff a future president needs to know,* she thought eagerly.

She picked up her notebook and turned to Aurora. "I didn't meet any assassins," she said, "but I did have an adventure."

"No joke?" Aurora glanced over her shoulder at Marissa and Elizabeth. "Hey, you guys," she called, "let's walk to our next class together. I need moral support."

"Why? What's next?" Lindsay asked.

"Physical Education," Aurora said with a grimace.

"PE?" Marissa gasped, running over to join them. "Oh no! I look horrible in athletic shoes!"

"They didn't have PE in my old school," Elizabeth said, hugging her notebook to her chest. "Just calisthenics in homeroom every morning."

"What school did you go to?" Lindsay asked.

Elizabeth looked away. "You wouldn't have heard of it."

"So what's this adventure you had?" Aurora asked as the four girls headed out of Ms. Iver's class.

Lindsay paused, letting the suspense build. Then she said, "I met a boy in the bathroom."

Aurora gasped and Elizabeth turned white. Marissa let out a squeal. "Oh, my gosh! I would just die!"

"I practically did," Lindsay said. "But he turned out to be a nice guy. His name is Henry Bartholomew and he's in 6-B. He's known Chas Randall since they were little kids, and they can't stand each other."

"Chas is really popular, you know," Marissa remarked, running her fingers through her flouncy curls. "He's only a sixth grader like us, and already everyone wants to hang out with him."

"That's no surprise," Aurora said disdainfully. "I mean, his family practically owns the school."

"So?"

"So just because a person's got hotshot relatives doesn't mean he's something special."

Marissa rolled her eyes, but Aurora just shrugged and walked out of Founder's Hall into the morning sunlight. The paths were crowded with boys talking and calling to one another as they headed for their next class. They stared at the girls, and then put their heads together and snickered.

"Where's the gymnasium?" Lindsay wondered aloud, ignoring the boys as she checked her map. "It's not on the quad with the other buildings."

"I thought you'd know your way around," Marissa said. "Didn't Mr. Bertozzi say your brother goes here?"

"I've come here a few times to watch him play tennis, but that's all," Lindsay answered, feeling a little defensive. Was she supposed to be a Randall Hall expert just because her brother went to the school?

"The gym is over there," Elizabeth said, pointing across the grassy athletic fields that stretched out behind Founder's Hall. Unlike the other school buildings, the gym was a modern concrete structure with a flat roof and no windows. "I heard it's got a swimming pool and everything," she added.

Aurora turned to her. "But the important question is, does it have a girls' locker room?"

Elizabeth's eyes grew wide and Marissa gulped. Only Lindsay failed to react, and that was because she had just noticed Henry walking up the path.

"Hi, Lindsay," he called, strolling up to join them.

"Hi. This is Henry," she told the girls.

"Ah, yes, the boy who lurks in bathrooms," Aurora said with delight.

Henry grinned. "That's me."

Marissa gazed at Henry from under her long eyelashes. "Hi, Henry," she said in a breathy voice. "Lindsay says you know Chas."

Henry cleared his throat and laughed foolishly. "Yeah . . . uh, sure . . . we go way back." He shrugged, coughed, and stared at his feet.

Lindsay frowned. Henry was acting as if Marissa were a famous movie star or something. The thought annoyed her, but she wasn't sure why.

"You didn't get in trouble when you got back to class, did you, Lindsay?" Henry asked. "I mean, you and I were out in the hall a long time."

"No. Ms. Iver came out and Chas sucked up to her."

"Henry, could you introduce me to Chas sometime?" Marissa asked.

Henry didn't answer. He stared into Marissa's huge eyes, apparently paralyzed.

"Marissa, get with the program," Lindsay said disdainfully. "Henry and Chas are not best friends. They're enemies."

"I, uh, I could maybe introduce you sometime," Henry said quietly.

Lindsay let out an exasperated sigh. What was wrong with Henry? He'd taken one look at Marissa and turned from a hot chili pepper into a marshmallow. Admittedly, Marissa was pretty in a vacant sort of way, but Lindsay never would have guessed that Henry was the kind of kid who fell for that type. *Just shows how wrong you can be,* she thought with irritation.

The bell rang, jarring Lindsay out of her thoughts.

"We're late," Elizabeth gasped.

"Come on," Lindsay said, breaking into a run. "Bye, Henry."

"See you," he called, taking off in the opposite direction.

Lindsay was in the lead as they reached the gymnasium building. Breathing hard, she burst through the doors—and ran right into a huge man with a body full of muscles and a face like a bulldog. She bounced off his muscular chest like a Ping-Pong ball off a concrete wall. Reeling backward, she knocked into Aurora, who in turn backed into Elizabeth, who stumbled against Marissa. All four of them fell like bowling pins and landed in a heap on the floor.

"Are you all right?" a deep voice demanded.

Gasping for breath, Lindsay looked up into the man's face. "I . . . I think so," she panted.

The man held out his hand and pulled the girls to their feet like a gorilla lifting four rag dolls. "I'm Mr. Brack, your PE teacher," he bellowed. "You're late!"

"I'm sorry, we—" Aurora began.

"Even worse, you're out of shape. But we'll take care of that later." He crossed his beefy arms over his massive chest. "Now, listen up. There is no girls' locker room in the Charles Bennington Randall III Sports Center. Therefore, until other arrangements can be made, you will have to change in one of the equipment storage rooms. Follow me."

Like a general leading his troops into battle, he led the girls across the lobby and down a hallway to an unmarked door. Aurora caught Lindsay's eye and saluted. Lindsay stifled a giggle.

Taking a ring of keys out of his pocket, Mr. Brack

unlocked the door and flipped on the light. Lindsay peered around his bulging biceps into the room. It was about ten feet square, and every inch was filled with football equipment. There were stacks of blue-and-white football helmets, musty-smelling shoulder pads, grass-stained footballs, even piles of spiked football shoes.

"But this is a closet!" Marissa cried. "I can't get dressed in a closet. There's no mirror!"

"I don't think there's enough room, Mr. Brack," Lindsay ventured.

"Besides, it smells like stinky sweat socks," Aurora said, holding her nose.

"Sorry," Mr. Brack said. Lindsay didn't think he sounded very sincere. "It's the best we can do for now. Just toss the equipment into the corner. I left you four gym uniforms, size small."

Marissa gazed suspiciously at the neatly folded pile of gym clothes that lay on one of the stacks of shoulder pads. She picked up a uniform and opened it. It consisted of blue shorts, white socks, and a white T-shirt with the words RANDALL HALL printed across the front. "But these are *boys'* gym uniforms," she said with dismay.

"That's all we've got," Mr. Brack replied. "Now get moving. I'll expect you in the gym in exactly five minutes." With that, he turned and walked away.

"Five minutes!" Marissa exclaimed when he was out of sight. "I've never gotten dressed in less than a half hour in my entire life."

"You must have been the best-dressed toddler on the playground," Aurora said sarcastically. "Come on, let's move this junk and get going."

Gingerly, Lindsay picked up a set of grimy shoulder pads and tossed them into the corner. The other girls joined in, and soon they had emptied a space just big enough for the four of them to walk into the closet and close the door. They stood there, elbow to elbow, avoiding one another's eyes.

"I've never gotten undressed in front of anyone except my mother and my sisters," Elizabeth admitted.

"Me, neither," Marissa said.

Lindsay nodded. At her house, everyone was very private. Her mother and father even had separate bathrooms.

"Oh, what's the big deal?" Aurora asked. "Haven't you ever been skinny-dipping?"

"No," Lindsay answered with surprise, "have you?"

"Sure. When my father finished filming *Deadly Mission II,* there was a big cast party at the director's house. At midnight someone pushed the producer into the pool, and pretty soon everyone was taking off their clothes and jumping in."

"Your father was in *Deadly Mission II?*" Elizabeth said with awe. "Who is he?"

"Burton Barkley," she said. "No one knows his name, but everyone recognizes his face. He's a character actor. He usually plays smooth-talking bad guys."

"Don't be too impressed, Elizabeth," Marissa said sarcastically. "Just because a person's got hotshot relatives doesn't mean she's something special."

"Oh, good one," Aurora said disdainfully as she slipped out of her baggy turquoise dress.

She didn't seem the least bit embarrassed, so Lindsay

gathered up her courage and began to undress, too. Soon Marissa and Elizabeth were doing the same. It wasn't easy in such a tiny space, and everyone got poked in the ribs by someone else's elbow at least once. During one of those times, Lindsay sneaked a peek at the other girls. Like her, Aurora was wearing a bra, and also like her, she didn't need to. Marissa, on the other hand, filled out her bra quite well, while Elizabeth still wore an undershirt.

"I can't go out there in this," Marissa wailed as she wiggled into her T-shirt and shorts. "My hips look gigantic!"

"Oh, get a grip," Aurora snapped. "You're gorgeous and you know it. I'm so shapeless, I'll probably be mistaken for a long-haired boy."

"Well, at least you don't have ostrich legs," Lindsay complained, staring down at her long legs and bony knees.

"I can barely *see* my legs," Elizabeth said. Her baggy T-shirt covered her rear end, and her shorts hung down almost to her knees.

Suddenly, there was a loud knock at the door. The girls jumped, cracking elbows. "Who is it?" Lindsay asked.

"Mr. Brack sent me to get you," a familiar voice said. "You're late."

"It's Chas," Lindsay said with disgust.

"*Aakk!*" Marissa shrieked. "I can't let him see me like this!"

"So what are you going to do?" Aurora asked. "Hide in here all period?" She opened the door.

Chas was standing there in his gym uniform looking tall and handsome. He took one look at the girls and burst out laughing.

41

"I know we look dorky, but give us a break, will you, Chas?" Lindsay asked, remembering Ms. Iver's lecture about coming on too strong. "We're just trying to fit in."

"Oh, don't make me laugh," Chas shot back. "You don't want to fit in. If it were up to you, you'd come to gym class in hot pink aerobics leotards."

"That's not true," Lindsay argued. "We just want to be ordinary Randall Hall students, but you boys won't let us."

"Then why did you come to school in fancy dresses?" he demanded.

"Mr. Bertozzi told us to wear dresses or skirts," Elizabeth said shyly.

Chas scowled. "Sure, blue and white dresses maybe, but you came dressed like a bunch of peacocks. I think you just like to show off."

"Well, I *do* like to look nice," Marissa said with a coy smile.

"What I want to know is, why does *anyone* have to wear uniforms?" Aurora asked. "Public school kids can wear whatever they want." She pushed past Chas and started down the hall toward the gym. The other girls followed.

"Because it's in the rule book, that's why," Chas said, bringing up the rear. "Besides, it's Randall Hall tradition, passed down from my great-great grandfather through the generations. But you girls wouldn't understand that," he added pompously.

Lindsay heard the smoke alarm in her brain go off. *Chas is so full of himself!* she thought furiously. *If I had one of those magic fireballs, I'd drop it down his gym shorts!*

"Chas Randall," she began, pushing open the door to the gym, "what makes you think—"

"Girls, you are three minutes late!" Mr. Brack roared. He was standing in front of the bleachers with his hands on his hips. In front of him, five rows of boys were standing at attention. "Three laps around the gym!" he yelled. "One for each minute. Hup! Hup!"

"Have a nice run, girls," Chas chuckled as he strolled over to join the boys.

With a groan, Lindsay, Aurora, Marissa, and Elizabeth began jogging around the edge of the gym. The boys, who were now sitting cross-legged on the floor while Mr. Brack talked, watched with obvious delight.

"This is a nightmare," Marissa whined. "I'm getting all sweaty."

"Oh, shut up and run," Aurora snapped.

"You shut up," Marissa shot back. "If you hadn't gotten into an argument with Chas, we would have been here on time."

"Puh-leeze! If it were up to you, you would have thrown him down on the football helmets and kissed him!"

Lindsay was only half listening. She had just had an incredible idea. "Listen," she breathed. "Chas thinks we don't care about Randall Hall tradition, right? Well, what if we came to school dressed exactly like the boys—blazers, slacks, white shirts, even ties? Then Chas couldn't possibly accuse us of showing off."

"I don't think Mr. Bertozzi would approve," Elizabeth said anxiously.

"If he wants us to follow the Randall Hall rule book, he'll have to," Aurora said eagerly. "Besides, if he freaks, it'll give us a perfect opening to point out that uniforms are antihuman, anticreative—and totally uncool."

"Yeah," said Lindsay, but her mind was wandering. What if her brilliant idea turned out to be a disaster? After all, Ms. Iver had told her to stop sticking out like a sore thumb and try fitting in. *But in a way, that's exactly what we'd be doing,* she reassured herself. And then there was Fraser to consider. If she embarrassed him again, he'd probably give her a noogie concussion. On the other hand, Fraser constantly complained about having to wear a uniform. *If I could convince the school to dump the uniform rule, he'd be on cloud nine,* she told herself.

"Well," Aurora panted as they rounded the gym for lap three, "what do you think? Should we do it?"

"But I don't *want* to dress like a boy," Marissa argued.

"Look at it this way," Lindsay said. "If Chas decides to complain to Mr. Bertozzi about our colorful clothes, the school will probably force us to wear blue skirts and white blouses every day. But if we can convince the school to drop the uniform rule, you'll be able to wear whatever you want."

"Well . . ."

"Oh, lighten up, you guys," Aurora said. "I mean, if the teachers are calling us Randy's Raiders, we might as well live up to our name, right?"

"Right!" Lindsay chimed in. She turned to Marissa. "Will you do it?"

"I guess so," she said reluctantly. "But just for one day."

"How about you, Elizabeth?" Aurora asked. "Are you with us?"

Elizabeth bit her lip. Her dark eyes darted left and right. "Well . . . okay," she said finally.

Lindsay grinned, ignoring her aching lungs and rubbery legs. "I can snitch some Randall Hall ties from my brother's closet," she said as the girls rounded the last corner of the gym. "All you three have to do is come to school in a blue blazer, blue pants, and a white blouse."

The girls nodded. Up ahead, Mr. Brack was waiting for them. Lindsay wiped her sweaty brow as she staggered to a halt in front of him. All she could think about was how good it was going to feel to sit down.

But Mr. Brack had other ideas. "Nice job, girls," he said with a nod. "Now grab a drink of water and hit the field. You're about to learn how to play touch football."

*L*indsay's alarm buzzed and her eyes fluttered open. Butterflies were frolicking in her stomach, and for a moment she didn't know why. Then she remembered. It was the second day of school—the day the girls were showing up in Randall Hall uniforms.

Lindsay closed her eyes and slipped into her favorite fantasy. She imagined it was twenty-five years in the future and she was running for president. Naturally, all the important national magazines—*Time, Newsweek, People, Ms.*—would write articles about her life. In her fantasy she opened *People* and started to read. . . .

Even as far back as middle school, Lindsay Tavish was making waves. In her first week at Randall Hall, she convinced the girl students to dress in male uniforms, thus inciting a riot and leading to her expulsion from the school.

Lindsay's eyes popped open. No, no, that was all wrong! She stared at the swirls of color on her quilt and let her mind drift off again. . . .

Lindsay Tavish has always been a leader, a rebel, a visionary. Perhaps it all started in middle school when she led the female students in a well-organized protest that led to a total rethinking of school policies and to her eventual election as president of the student council.

"Ah," Lindsay said, "that's more like it." Eagerly, she hopped out of bed—and let out a groan. Thanks to the grueling touch football game she had played in PE class yesterday, every muscle in her body ached. Maybe it wouldn't have been so bad, she decided, if Chas hadn't been on her team. He was constantly passing the ball to her, which meant that all the boys on the opposing team then ran her down and thumped her on the back with all their might.

With a weary sigh Lindsay put on her robe and limped into the hall. She could hear her mother and father talking in the kitchen downstairs. She tiptoed to Fraser's room. It was empty and the bathroom door at the end of the hall was closed. *Good,* she thought. *Considering how long Fraser stays in the shower, this should be a cinch.*

She walked into his room and opened his closet. A half dozen Randall Hall ties were draped haphazardly over a hanger. She grabbed four and turned to leave.

"Lindsay?"

Lindsay stuffed the ties in her pocket and spun around. Mrs. Tavish, wearing a gray knit suit and white silk blouse, her auburn hair pulled back in a bun, was standing in the doorway. "What are you doing in Fraser's room?" she asked.

"Uh . . . returning a book I borrowed." She smiled, trying to look innocent. "What's up, Mom?"

"You have a telephone call," her mother said. She walked closer and brushed a stray lock of hair from Lindsay's cheek as if she were centering a vase of flowers on the mantelpiece. "Don't stay on long. The final bids on the new hospital wing are due today, and I'm expecting a call from an architectural firm in Tokyo."

"Okay." Lindsay went into her mother's bedroom and picked up the phone. "Hello?"

"Lindsay?" a small voice said. "It's me, Elizabeth."

"What's up?" Lindsay asked, nervously wondering if Elizabeth had blabbed the plan to her parents, who had called Mr. Bertozzi, who had called the Board of Trustees, who had . . .

"I don't have a blue blazer."

"Well, why didn't you borrow one, or buy one at a thrift shop or something?"

"I didn't . . . I couldn't . . ." Her voice trailed off. "I'm sorry. I've ruined everything."

"No, you haven't. Look, I'll see if I can sneak one from my brother's closet. It'll be much too big, but it's better than nothing."

"Oh, Lindsay," Elizabeth said gratefully, "would you?"

"Sure." She frowned. "I just hope Aurora and Marissa don't chicken out."

"They won't. And even if they do, at least you and I will be dressed the same."

Now it was Lindsay's turn to feel grateful. "Thanks,

Elizabeth," she said with a smile. "See you soon."

Lindsay was crouching behind an azalea bush at the corner of the auditorium, anxiously watching the parking lot. Randall Hall School didn't have buses, which meant the kids had to be dropped off by their parents. Slowly, a caravan of cars wound through the parking lot. Each car stopped in front of the auditorium, deposited one or more boys, and then drove away.

Lindsay noticed something moving in the quad. Pressing herself deeper into the bushes, she saw Mr. Bertozzi walk out of the school office and stroll over to a large, well-manicured flower bed. In the center of the flower bed, the words RANDALL HALL were spelled out in blue and white flowers. Mr. Bertozzi paused to slip on a pair of gardening gloves. Then he knelt down and began clearing the flower bed of weeds and fallen leaves.

Don't they have gardeners to do that? Lindsay wondered. She watched Mr. Bertozzi curiously until she noticed Aurora getting out of a pale green Range Rover. She was wearing designer jeans and a white tuxedo shirt, and carrying a blue blazer over her arm.

"*Psst!*" Lindsay hissed. "Over here!"

Aurora looked around blankly, and then caught sight of Lindsay. "Hi!" she called, hurrying to join her. "Did you get the ties?"

"Yes, but I didn't want Fraser to know what was going on, so I wore a white blouse and a skirt to school and stuffed everything else in my backpack. Then I changed here in the bushes."

Aurora laughed. "Pretty bold. It won't be long before

you're ready to go skinny-dipping."

"Well, what do you think?" a lilting voice asked.

Lindsay and Aurora looked up to see Marissa standing in front of them. She was wearing skin-tight navy blue leggings, a lacy white blouse, and a blue velvet jacket.

"Marissa, we're supposed to be fitting in," Lindsay said with dismay.

"Well, that doesn't mean we have to look ugly, does it?" Marissa asked.

Just then the warning bell rang. Lindsay looked around. The parking lot was almost empty. A group of boys who were sitting on the front steps got up and went inside. "Where's Elizabeth?" she asked anxiously.

"There she is," Marissa said, pointing across the parking lot. Elizabeth, wearing a white blouse and a gray skirt, was walking quickly down the driveway.

"Over here," Aurora called. Elizabeth jogged over. "What were you doing on the other side of the parking lot?" Aurora asked. "Didn't your parents drive you?"

"Sure they did," Elizabeth answered, looking away. "I just . . . I was just looking for you guys, that's all."

"Where are your blue pants?" Lindsay asked.

With a small smile, Elizabeth lifted up her skirt to reveal a pair of blue slacks rolled up to the knees. Quickly she unrolled the slacks and took off her skirt. Lindsay handed her one of Fraser's blazers and she put it on. The arms hung down below her fingertips.

"I just realized something," Lindsay confessed, holding up four striped ties. "I have no idea how to tie these things."

"I do," Elizabeth said. "I have two little brothers, and I

have to help them get ready for church every Sunday." With sure hands she slipped a tie around each girl's neck and knotted it.

The girls looked at one another. Despite their mismatched clothing, their outfits looked remarkably like Randall Hall uniforms.

"Yuck," Marissa groaned, "we all look alike."

"That's the point, you dope," Aurora said.

"Don't call me a dope, you flake!" Marissa shot back.

"Come *on*," Lindsay broke in, grabbing their arms and dragging them toward the auditorium. "It's now or never."

Together, the four girls ran up the stairs. Ignoring the pounding of her heart, Lindsay threw open the door and stepped inside. She paused, glancing quickly around the noisy auditorium. The only empty seats were in the front row. With a glance to make sure the other girls were behind her, she started up the aisle.

At that exact moment the final bell rang and the auditorium fell silent. Mr. Bertozzi stepped up to the podium and opened his mouth to speak. Then he caught sight of the girls. His mouth fell open and his eyes grew wide. "Wha—what in the world?" he stammered.

Every boy in the room turned around and stared. Some of them laughed. Some of them booed. The room buzzed with whispers, which soon turned into noisy talking and shouting.

Lindsay wiped her damp palms against her blue blazer. She had figured that wearing Randall Hall uniforms would cause a stir, but this was more than even she had bargained for. She glanced at the boys' faces, trying to gauge their reaction. Most of them looked more surprised than anything else. *But what about Mr. Bertozzi?* she wondered.

"What is the meaning of this?" he bellowed as the girls sat down. His lips were pressed into a thin, straight line.

Lindsay swallowed hard. "Well . . . uh . . . we didn't feel comfortable wearing ordinary clothes when all the other students were in uniforms."

"So we decided to follow tradition and wear uniforms, too," Aurora piped up.

Chas jumped to his feet. "If you wanted to follow tradition, you wouldn't be at Randall Hall at all!" he cried. A few boys cheered and applauded. Chas turned to Mr. Bertozzi. "If you ask me, they're just dressing like that to get attention."

"I am not," Marissa said indignantly. "If I wanted to get your attention, I'd wear something pretty—not pants and an ugly striped tie."

The boys laughed—all except Chas, who rolled his eyes and groaned.

"This has nothing to do with showing off," Lindsay said. "What we're trying to do is fit in." She reached into her blazer pocket and pulled out the official Randall Hall rule book that the school had sent her with her acceptance letter. "It says right here on page 4: 'All Randall Hall students shall wear blue slacks, official school blazers, and white shirts with official school ties.'" She shrugged. "Well, we're Randall Hall students, aren't we? What goes for the boys should go for us, too."

The boys laughed. There was a smattering of applause, and someone yelled, "Way to go, girls!"

Lindsay saw Chas looking to Mr. Bertozzi for support, but the headmaster seemed stunned. He opened and closed his mouth a few times, but no words came out. Chas scowled. "But they aren't wearing *official* blazers and ties," he pointed out.

"I am," Elizabeth piped up. "Lindsay snitched my blazer and the ties from her brother. Oops!" she cried, turning red. "I guess wasn't supposed to say that."

Everyone burst out laughing. Lindsay scanned the crowd until she found Fraser. The boys around him were laughing and poking him. Lindsay met his eye and smiled apologetically. He looked away.

"The girls have brought up an important point," Ms. Iver said, getting to her feet. "The rule book was written when this was an all-boys' school. Either we need to supply the girls with official uniforms, or we need to rewrite the rules."

"I say we ought to rewrite the rules," Aurora said, turning to face the boys. "Why do we need to wear uniforms?"

The majority of the boys let out a spontaneous cheer. Some of them looked startled, and a few—including Chas—looked outraged.

Lindsay noticed that most of the teachers seemed outraged, too. "Are you suggesting that the students be allowed to wear whatever they please?" demanded Mr. Wardlaw, the girls' math teacher.

Henry jumped to his feet. "Why not? After all, this isn't a military school."

"That's right," Lindsay added, flipping through the rule book. "And it says right here in the section on Randall

Hall's purpose and philosophy, 'Randall Hall views each student as a unique individual with his own individual contributions to make.' Well, isn't what I wear part of my individuality?"

The boys cheered and stomped their feet.

"That is enough!" Mr. Bertozzi shouted. The auditorium fell silent. "My job is to enforce the rules, not to make them. If you want the school to consider abolishing the dress code, you will have to take your request to the Board of Trustees. Now, I have a few announcements to make."

Mr. Bertozzi spent the next five minutes reading announcements about soccer practice, glee club tryouts, and the first lacrosse game of the season. Then he put down his notes and said, "Now, Chas Randall will continue his talk about Randall Hall's history and traditions."

Chas walked to the podium and smiled. "This morning I'd like to tell all the sixth graders about a tradition that was started by my great-uncle Benjamin Randall back in 1934. Every year someone in the sixth-grade class dresses up the statue of Charles Bennington Randall in the courtyard. The idea is to do it when no one is looking and surprise everyone. My great-uncle put a jack-o'-lantern on the statue's head. Since then the statue's been dressed in everything from a Santa Claus hat to bunny ears."

"It's a delightful tradition," Mr. Bertozzi said with a smile. "But please, do not deface the statue in any way. And if you are caught skipping class to dress the statue, you will be—"

The bell rang, drowning out Mr. Bertozzi's final words. The girls leaped to their feet and headed for the door. Lindsay saw Henry waiting for them. "You were outstanding!" he exclaimed. "Chas was furious!"

Lindsay laughed, but her mind was on Fraser. Where was he? She had to talk to him and apologize for taking his clothes.

Just then Chas and three other boys walked up to the girls. "If you think you're going to change the dress code, forget it," Chas said. "There are five people on the Board of Trustees—and three of them are my relatives."

"Oh, man! He really *does* own the school," Aurora moaned.

"Hey, Peanut," Chas said, turning to Henry. "What class do you have next?"

"Social Studies. Why?"

"Because your Social Studies book is missing." Chas grabbed the book from under Henry's arm and ran across the quad to the flower bed where the words RANDALL HALL were spelled out in blue and white flowers. A few passing boys stopped to watch as Chas flung Henry's book into the center of the flowers. His friends cheered.

Henry and the girls ran over to the edge of the flower bed. The book was lying in the middle of the D, pinning down a patch of white flowers. Henry took a tentative step into the flower bed.

"I wouldn't do that if I were you," said a tall boy with olive skin and black hair who had stopped to watch. "Mr. Bertozzi planted that garden himself, and he's wacko about it."

"Oh, now I understand why I saw him working in it this morning," Lindsay said.

The tall boy nodded. "I'm telling you, he loves those flowers. Last year someone threw a Frisbee in there by accident and Mr. B. was so mad, he made the kid weed the garden for the rest of the school year."

"Well, it's not Henry who's going to get in trouble if Mr. Bertozzi shows up," Aurora pointed out. "Chas threw the book."

"Oh, yeah?" Chas said. "Who do you think Mr. Bertozzi's going to believe, Mr. Peanut or me?"

Henry hesitated.

That Chas is such a bully! Lindsay thought furiously. "I'm not afraid of Chas *or* Mr. Bertozzi," she said impetuously. With that she tiptoed into the flower bed, grabbed Henry's book, and hopped out. The girls cheered, and even some of the boys applauded.

"Excellent!" Henry cried, slapping palms with Lindsay as she handed him the book.

"Pretty bold," Chas said grudgingly. "But let's see if you're bold enough—and clever enough—to dress up my great-great-grandfather's statue before my friends and I do."

Lindsay didn't answer. The reality of what she had just done was starting to hit her. Her heart pounded and her palms grew damp. She glanced around nervously, wondering if Mr. Bertozzi or one of the other teachers had seen her.

Aurora answered Chas for her. "You're on, Chas Randall!" she said. "We'll dress up that statue faster *and* better than any sixth graders in the history of the school!"

A moment later the bell rang. As everyone turned to go, Lindsay noticed Ms. Iver standing at the corner of the school office building. With a panicky feeling, she realized her teacher must have seen her jump into the flower bed. *I'm in big trouble,* Lindsay thought.

But as their eyes met, Ms. Iver smiled slightly and turned away. Lindsay's heart soared. Ms. Iver understood.

*A*re we really going to do it?" Elizabeth asked as the girls carried their lunch trays into the crowded cafeteria that afternoon. "Are we going to dress up the statue?"

"Of course we are," Aurora said. She paused uncertainly as the boys turned to stare at them. "Hey, where do you want to sit?"

Lindsay glanced around the room. Unlike most public school lunchrooms, the Randall Hall cafeteria had oak tables with high-backed oak chairs and a hand-painted mural on the wall showing the school as it had looked when it was Charles Bennington Randall's estate.

Most of the tables were already taken. Lindsay noticed Chas sitting at the head of a table next to the window. He was talking while the rest of the boys listened with rapt attention.

"Let's sit there," Marissa said eagerly, pointing to an empty table next to Chas.

Lindsay knew that any table Chas chose had to be in the section where the popular kids sat. "I don't want anyone to accuse us of showing off," Lindsay said, remembering the expression on her brother's face during Assembly. "Let's just take a table in the back."

"No way," Aurora insisted. "Once we pick a table we'll be stuck there for the rest of the year. Come on." She walked to the empty table next to Chas and sat down. Marissa and Elizabeth hurried after her.

Reluctantly Lindsay joined them. She glanced over at Chas. He was pointedly ignoring them.

"What are we going to do about the statue?" Elizabeth asked.

"I've got an idea," Aurora whispered, leaning close so the boys wouldn't hear. "Did you ever hear that corny old song from the sixties, 'Where the Boys Are'? It's from a beach movie starring Connie Francis. We could put Charlie in a bikini and rig up a tape recorder to play the title song over and over!"

But Lindsay shook her head. "The boys will think we're pushing the whole feminist thing in their faces again. If we want them to accept us, we have to stick to tradition."

"I hate tradition," Aurora groaned. "It's so old-fashioned, so boring, so . . . traditional."

"Chas said his great-uncle put a jack-o'-lantern on the statue," Elizabeth said. "Maybe we could do that."

"Bo-ring," Marissa replied. "Hey," she cried, perking up. "I've got another idea. I heard that Chas is going to try out for the basketball team. What if we dressed the statue as a Randall Hall basketball player?"

"Basketball is okay, but a football uniform would look even better," Lindsay said. She smiled a knowing smile. "And gym class is next period. All we have to do is borrow a few things from the equipment closet."

"But when will we dress the statue?" Elizabeth asked.

"After school?" Marissa suggested.

Lindsay shook her head. "Did you hear all those announcements Mr. Bertozzi made about after-school activities? There'll be too many kids around."

Aurora's eyes grew wide. "I've got it! The whole school attends Assembly, right? Let's skip tomorrow morning and dress up Charlie. Then when Assembly ends, everyone will come out of the auditorium and see him."

"I think people will notice if all four of us are missing at Assembly," Elizabeth pointed out.

"Okay, so just two of us will do it," Aurora replied. "And we don't have to skip. We can say we're sick and get excused." She picked up her fork and poked tentatively at the odd-looking yellow stew on her plate. "Hey, what is this stuff? It looks like dog food."

"According to the menu, it's Founder's Stew," Elizabeth said.

Lindsay giggled. "Maybe every year they dig up Charles Bennington Randall's body and chop off another little bit to put in the stew."

"Ew, gross!" Marissa cried, pushing away her tray.

"I'm a vegetarian," Aurora said. "I don't eat anything that used to have a face, especially old Charlie's face."

"Did you know this building used to be Charles Randall's stable?" Lindsay said, wrinkling her nose. "Maybe that lumpy stuff is actually horse meat!"

The girls let out a collective shriek and burst out laughing.

"Excuse me, girls," a boy's voice said from somewhere above Lindsay's head. She looked up and found herself gazing into the face of a hulking brown-eyed boy. Out of the corner of her eye, she could see four or five other boys standing on either side of him. The boy grinned, exposing a mouth full of silver braces, and said, "This table is taken."

Lindsay tried to turn her body around to face the boy directly, but he was leaning up against her chair, pinning her to the table. "What are you talking about?" she demanded. "The table was empty when we got here."

"But there are still plenty of seats," Marissa added with a shake of her curls. "You're welcome to join us."

"Maybe you don't understand," the boy said in a tone of voice most people reserve for talking to tiny, drooling babies. "This table is reserved for the quarterback of the football team and his friends."

Lindsay gazed up at him. He smiled back menacingly, like a barracuda with braces. "And guess what?" he said. "I'm Will Dalton, the quarterback."

Before Lindsay could answer, he grabbed the back of her chair and hoisted her high into the air. Lindsay gasped and clutched the seat. The entire cafeteria burst out laughing.

"Put me down!" Lindsay cried.

Instead, Will's buddies lifted Aurora, Marissa, and

Elizabeth into the air, too. Lindsay looked around for a teacher who might save them, but all she saw was Chas and his friends, laughing and cheering loudly.

"Throw 'em out!" Chas shouted.

"Let's really punish them," someone else yelled. "Make them eat our Founder's Stew!"

Laughing raucously, Will and his pals carried the girls across the cafeteria and put them down at an empty table in the corner. Two other boys carried their lunch trays over and dropped them onto the table. "Have a good lunch, girls," Will said with a smile. Then he and his friends picked up some empty chairs, strolled back to the table by the window, and sat down.

An instant later the lunch monitors, Ms. Iver and Mr. Brack, walked in and gazed around the noisy, laughing lunchroom.

"Where were they when we needed them?" Elizabeth muttered.

"I don't know, but they're here now and I'm telling," Aurora said, getting to her feet.

But Lindsay had just noticed Fraser sitting at a nearby table. He was talking and laughing with his friends, and for the first time since school started, he looked happy. "Forget it," she said, grabbing Aurora's arm. "Let's show the boys we can take a joke."

"But—" Aurora began.

"Don't worry. We'll get our revenge tomorrow when we decorate old Charlie. We can dress him up in Will Dalton's football jersey and a girdle!"

"It's a deal," Aurora said, taking a seat.

Lindsay caught her brother's eye and smiled. He

grinned back. Then she gritted her teeth and dug into her Founder's Stew.

The next morning Lindsay, Aurora, Marissa, and Elizabeth huddled together behind the azalea bush at the corner of the auditorium, finalizing their plans. At their feet lay a Randall Hall football helmet, shoulder pads, a jersey, and a football, all borrowed from the equipment room at the gym. On the top of the pile was a girdle—size humongous—that Aurora had purchased at a thrift shop the night before. She had cut open the sides and had sewn Velcro strips on it to make it easier to put on the statue.

"Okay," Aurora said, "here's the plan: One of us fakes illness to get out of Assembly and then dresses the statue. The girls who stay inside have to do something to draw attention away from the windows. Got it?"

"But who dresses the statue?" Elizabeth asked.

"I figured we could draw straws," Lindsay answered, pulling a package of drinking straws out of her backpack. She had borrowed them from the pantry at home and had carefully cut one straw in half. "The one who gets the short straw dresses up Charlie." She clasped four straws in her hand so that only their ends were showing.

Each girl selected a straw and held it up. Lindsay's stomach did a back flip. She was left with the short straw!

"*Gracias a Dios*," Elizabeth whispered, glancing heavenward.

"Good luck, Lindsay," Marissa said with a grin.

"According to my mother's psychic, you make your own luck," Aurora said. "But this can help." She reached into her pocket and pulled out a crystal. "This crystal is full of spiritual energy. It's got awesome power. Just touch it and you're home free."

"Earth to Aurora, earth to Aurora," Marissa said sarcastically. "It's time to return to reality."

"Hey, you guys have a job to do, too, you know," Lindsay broke in. "You have to distract the boys so no one looks out the auditorium windows and sees me."

"And, no," Aurora added, looking straight at Marissa, "tossing your hair around and giggling will not do the trick."

Marissa rolled her eyes disdainfully. "I can fake a great coughing fit. I do it all the time at my grandmother's house. My big sister hates veal, so when Nannie makes cutlets, I pretend to choke and Tina tosses her veal to the dog."

"Perfect," Lindsay said as the bell rang. Aurora held out the crystal and Lindsay took it. *It can't hurt*, she thought. Then, ignoring the fluttering in her stomach, she said, "Let's go."

As the girls walked into the auditorium, Lindsay reached up and nervously straightened her Randall Hall tie. Except for Marissa, who had on a short pink dress and white boots, the girls were still wearing their version of the Randall Hall uniform. It had been Aurora's idea to continue wearing uniforms. She had talked to Ms. Iver after English class yesterday and convinced her to help them present their "no uniforms" proposal to the Board of Trustees.

"Until the trustees vote on the uniform rule," Aurora had told the girls, "we have to dress just like the boys."

"But why?" Marissa had asked.

"It draws attention to the problem," Aurora had told her. "Besides, it's a sign of solidarity with the guys."

"I don't want to show solidarity with the guys," Marissa had argued. "I want to show them I'm a girl."

So Marissa had returned to wearing dresses, while the other girls stuck with their makeshift uniforms. Lindsay sighed, remembering how nervous she had felt asking Fraser to let her borrow his ties and blazer for a few more days. Naturally, he had given her a hard time, putting her down for sneaking into his room and teasing her about the way Will Dalton carried her across the dining hall. In the end he had agreed to lend her the ties and jacket, providing she did all his chores—including taking out the garbage and raking the leaves—for the next two weeks.

The final bell rang, bringing Lindsay back to the moment. While the other girls took seats at the far side of the auditorium, away from the quadrangle, she walked up to the podium where Mr. Bertozzi was glancing through the morning announcements.

"Excuse me, Mr. Bertozzi," she began, "I don't feel well."

He glanced up from his papers and frowned disapprovingly at her clothes. "What did you say?"

"I . . . can I be excused?"

"Excused? Why?"

"Why?" she repeated foolishly. She hadn't expected Mr. Bertozzi to ask so many questions. "Well, I . . . I'm sick."

He gazed down at her suspiciously. *Can he read my mind?* she wondered. *Does he know what I'm going to do?*

The seconds ticked by. "What exactly is the problem?" he asked at last.

Suddenly, Lindsay had an inspiration. "I'm having menstrual cramps," she blurted out.

Mr. Bertozzi cleared his throat and shuffled his papers. "Oh, my," he muttered. "Well, of course . . . naturally . . ." He waved his hand toward the door. "Go. *Go!*"

Stifling a giggle, Lindsay hurried out of the auditorium. She collected the football gear from under the azalea bush and jogged into the quad. Fortunately, there was no one in sight.

Glancing nervously at the auditorium windows, Lindsay hurried up to the statue of Charles Bennington Randall that stood in front of the library. It was even bigger than she remembered—ten feet tall, she estimated, with a concrete base that added another five feet or so.

Lindsay dropped the football equipment in the grass. Grabbing the girdle, she wrapped her arms around Charlie's legs and pulled herself up onto the base of the statue. She slid the girdle around the statue's waist and pressed the Velcro to hold it in place.

With her heart in her throat, she jumped down and picked up the football jersey. She climbed back onto the base of the statue and reached up to slip the jersey over Charlie's head. But it was hopeless. Even standing on tiptoe with her arms extended over her head, Lindsay couldn't reach higher than Charlie's shoulders.

What now? she wondered, trying to ignore the typhoon that was blowing in her stomach. She gazed up into Charles Bennington Randall's unsmiling face. Apparently he didn't realize how silly he looked in a girdle.

And then she had an idea. Charlie's left leg was slightly bent. If she could get a footing on his knee, she might be able to balance there long enough to get the football jersey and helmet on.

Quickly, she tied the jersey around her waist. There was no way to carry the helmet, so she put it on her head. Climbing onto the base of the statue, she reached up and put one hand on each of Charlie's shoulders. They felt sticky. Had some pigeons been using the statue as their bathroom? she wondered. It was a disgusting thought, but there was nothing she could do about it now. She pulled herself up until she was standing precariously with both feet on the statue's left knee.

Lindsay paused, trying to catch her breath. *Fraser could pull this off without breaking a sweat,* she thought. *But me—I'm the family klutz.* Still, she wasn't about to turn back now. Grasping Charlie's shoulder with her right hand, she reached down with her left hand and pulled the jersey from around her waist. As she did, her feet began to slip.

"*Yiieee!*" she cried. Letting the jersey drop, she threw both hands around Charlie's neck and flung her legs around his waist. She glanced down. The ground seemed very far below. Panic took over and she started shinnying up the statue. *If I can climb onto Charlie's shoulders, I'll be safe,* she told herself. Beyond that her mind was a blank.

Before she knew what had happened, she was sitting on the statue's shoulders, holding tight to Charlie's head. Sweat poured off her forehead and her breath came in short gasps. She forced herself to take one deep breath, then another and another. Gradually her panic subsided enough for her to realize she was going to be okay.

Lindsay smiled, suddenly aware of what had happened. Without even meaning to, she had maneuvered herself into the perfect position to put the football helmet on Charlie's head. Then, she told herself, she could climb down and retrieve the jersey.

Lindsay reached up to take the helmet from her own head and fit it on the statue. Then she heard it. A distant banging. She froze and looked toward the auditorium. Chas Randall was at one of the windows, tapping the pane with his knuckles. She heard his muffled shouts, and then suddenly the windows were filled with boys—dozens of boys—all pointing and laughing at her.

Lindsay went hot all over. Her heart kicked into overdrive. Without stopping to think, she began to scramble off Charlie's shoulders. But something was wrong. The seat of her thin cotton pants was stuck to the statue. In her panic Lindsay grabbed the waist of her pants and leaped to the ground.

R-r-r-r-r-i-i-p-p-p! She hit the grass and reached back to feel the seat of her pants. There was nothing there but her underwear!

With the football helmet still on her head and both hands on her rear end, Lindsay jumped to her feet. Then she took off running, and she didn't stop until she was locked inside the library bathroom.

*L*indsay, can you hear me?" Aurora called
through the door of the library bathroom.

Lindsay was sitting on the toilet, still wearing her
shredded pants. The borrowed football helmet was lying
on the floor where she'd tossed it. "Go away," she muttered.

"Lindsay, you've been in there a zillion years," Marissa
called. "Aren't you *ever* coming out?"

"Never. I'm going to grow old and die here."

"Very funny," Aurora said. "Come on, what's the big
deal? So most of Randall Hall School saw your underpants. So what?"

"So what?" Lindsay cried. "Aurora, you know that
crystal you made me carry? I'd like to stick it up your
nose!"

The next voice Lindsay heard belonged to Henry.
"Mr. Bertozzi tried to call your parents so they could

bring you a change of clothes, but your mom is in an emergency Board of Directors' meeting and your dad is in court."

"Boy, you must have really important parents," Elizabeth said with awe in her voice.

"But not to worry," Henry continued. "I brought you a pair of sweat pants from my gym locker. They're a little smelly, but otherwise fine."

Lindsay crossed her arms over her chest and stared at the white tile floor. How could she face the boys after what had happened? If it were up to her, she would crawl out the bathroom window, hitchhike to another state, and never show her face in Middleford, Pennsylvania, again.

"Lindsay," said a deep, rumbling voice, "this is Mr. Bertozzi."

Instinctively, Lindsay leaped up from the toilet. "Yes, sir," she called.

"While I sympathize with your feelings of embarrassment, I cannot condone the fact that you ignored a school rule by skipping Assembly to dress the statue. Furthermore, you are late to your first class. Consequently, if you do not come out of the bathroom within the next two minutes, I will be forced to give you a detention."

Lindsay gasped. She had never gotten a detention in her life, and she wasn't about to find out how her parents would react if she got one now. She quickly unlocked the door.

Instantly, the door flew open and Aurora, Marissa, and Elizabeth burst into the tiny bathroom. "Here," Elizabeth said, handing Lindsay a pair of faded navy blue sweat pants. "From Henry."

"What happened to you guys?" Lindsay demanded, unzipping her ripped pants. "I thought Marissa was supposed to throw a coughing fit and create a diversion."

"I did," Marissa said indignantly.

"Oh, sure," Aurora scoffed. "Three dainty coughs, and then she batted her eyelashes at the boy next to her and said, 'Excuse me, do you have a cough drop?' "

"Well, what did you expect me to do?" Marissa shot back. "Fall on the floor and throw an epileptic fit?"

"Look, it wouldn't have helped," Elizabeth said. "According to Henry, Chas is bragging to everyone how he tricked us. It turns out he overheard us in the dining hall talking about how we planned to dress the statue this morning. So he came to school early and coated the top half of old Charlie with slow-drying varnish."

"Varnish!" Lindsay cried. "No wonder my pants stuck."

Marissa giggled. "You looked so funny when you jumped off that statue . . ."

"Oh, thanks," Lindsay snapped, pulling off her slacks and stepping into Henry's overripe sweat pants. "Whose side are you on, anyway?"

"Hey, lighten up, Lindsay," Aurora said. "It didn't turn out so bad. Old Charlie looks pretty cute in his new girdle."

"But I wanted to dress the statue in a football uniform. I only suggested that stupid girdle to make you happy. Now everyone will think we're trying to throw the whole girl issue in their faces again."

"Maybe you should tell Mr. Bertozzi what Chas did," Elizabeth suggested.

"Are you kidding? Chas and Mr. Bertozzi are like this," Lindsay said, crossing her first two fingers. "They'd probably have a good laugh over what happened. Besides, I'm not a tattletale." She tucked her white blouse into the baggy sweatpants. It looked ridiculous. "Anyhow, none of this would have happened if you three hadn't screwed up."

"Hey, it's not our fault you drew the short straw," Marissa said. "I think Aurora's right. You need to lighten up."

"And *you* need to stop mooning over Chas Randall and get a life," Aurora shot back.

"Oh, shut up, you California raisin head," Marissa snapped.

Elizabeth let out a frustrated groan. "I knew we never should have tried to dress that silly statue in the first place."

"Well, why didn't you say something?" Lindsay asked irritably.

"Because I knew none of you would listen to me."

"Oh, come off it," Marissa cried, rolling her eyes. "You know, as soon as we met, I knew you were stuck up. 'I'm Elizabeth Lopez,'" she said, mimicking Elizabeth's speech on the first day of school. "'I'm Mexican-American, in case you couldn't tell.'"

Elizabeth looked as if she'd been slapped in the face. Her eyes grew wide and moist, and her lower lip began to tremble.

"Oh, Elizabeth, don't listen to her," Lindsay said. "She's just kidding around." But Elizabeth turned and ran out of the bathroom.

Aurora stared at Marissa with a look that would have frozen a volcano. "Nice work, Pea Brain."

"Don't call me Pea Brain, you Beverly Hills bubble head!"

"Oh, yeah, Pizza Breath? Why don't you—"

"Shut up, both of you!" Lindsay shouted, putting her hands over her ears. "Shut up, shut up, shut—"

"Young ladies," Mr. Bertozzi bellowed through the door, "get out of there this minute or you will all be suspended. I mean *now!*"

Lindsay, Aurora, and Marissa glared at one another. Without a word, they grabbed their books and stomped out of the rest room. Mr. Bertozzi was standing outside the door with his hands on his hips. He pointed silently at the library exit and they hurried through it.

The first thing Lindsay saw as she stepped outside was the statue of Charles Bennington Randall. Someone had taken the girdle off it and removed the football equipment from the grass. It was a little eerie, she thought. Almost as if she'd never begun to dress the statue at all. "Well, I sure *wish* I hadn't," she whispered to herself.

With a heavy heart, Lindsay started across the quad to Founder's Hall. As she walked, she glanced at Aurora and Marissa. Each girl was walking by herself, pointedly ignoring the other two.

Suddenly, a singsong voice floated through the air. "I saw London, I saw France, I saw Lindsay's underpants!"

Lindsay heard distant laugher, mixed with Aurora's and Marissa's giggles. She spun around, searching for the owner of the voice. But it could have come from any of the half-dozen partially opened windows in Founder's Hall.

Hot tears stung Lindsay's eyes. She turned and looked

back at the statue of Charles Bennington Randall. "I hate you," she whispered fiercely, "and I hate your rotten school, and your rotten great-great-grandson, too!" But old Charlie just stared straight ahead, completely unimpressed.

"How's school going?" Mr. Tavish asked as he drove Lindsay and Fraser to Randall Hall the next morning.

"It would be fine if only my adorable little sister would fall into a crack in the earth and disappear," Fraser said.

"What a thing to say!" Mr. Tavish exclaimed, but Lindsay could tell he was a little amused. "What did she do that's so terrible?"

"Yesterday she dressed up the statue of Charles Bennington Randall in a girdle!" he said with disgust.

Mr. Tavish chuckled. "Correct me if I'm wrong," he said, "but isn't it a Randall Hall tradition for the sixth graders to dress the statue?"

"Yeah, but why does it have to be *her?* And besides, her pants ripped and she—"

"This sounds like a fascinating story," Mr. Tavish interrupted as he pulled into the Randall Hall parking lot, "but can it wait until tonight? I'm late for court."

"No problem," Lindsay said quickly. So far she hadn't told her parents anything about her troubles at Randall Hall. After all, they had both been in situations where they had faced a hostile reception—her mom when she took over as director of Middleford County Hospital, and her father when he was first appointed judge—and both of them had charmed the socks off even their toughest critics. Her mother called it "grace under pressure," and even Fraser seemed to have a healthy dose of it.

I guess it runs in the family, Lindsay thought. *Only somehow I didn't get the gene.*

"Being one of the first girls at a boys' school is quite a challenge," Mr. Tavish said, almost as if he were reading her mind. "In fact, being the first one to step into new territory is always tough. People scrutinize your every move, just waiting for you to do something they can criticize."

Lindsay glanced down at her clothing. She had traded her makeshift Randall Hall uniform for a simple gray skirt and pale blue blouse. *They can scrutinize me all they want,* she thought. *From now on I'm not going to give them anything to criticize.*

It was all part of her new plan. Adapt or Die, she called it. From now on she wasn't going to let Chas or the other boys get to her. She was going to fit in, follow the rules, and keep smiling. In other words, she was going to learn to exhibit grace under pressure even if it killed her.

"Oh, school's not so bad," she lied, hopping out of the car. "Besides, we Tavishes love a good challenge." Fraser shot her a look of astonishment, but she ignored him and waved as her father drove away. Then she turned on her heels and strolled into the auditorium.

The first thing Lindsay noticed was Aurora sitting alone in the front row, still dressed in her unique version of the Randall Hall uniform. Marissa was sitting in the middle with Chas and his friends. She was wearing a short skirt, a fuzzy white sweater, and lipstick. Elizabeth was in the back, dressed in the same skirt and blouse she'd worn the first day, with her head stuck in a book.

Lindsay was wondering whether to sit with one of the girls or take a seat in the nearest empty row when she saw Henry waving to her. Gratefully, she hurried down the aisle and sat beside him.

"Hey, what's up?" he asked. "Why aren't you girls sitting together?"

She shrugged. She didn't want to talk about their fight in the library bathroom. *Anyway, it's probably for the best,* she told herself. *Except for being girls, we don't have anything in common.* "We'll never be accepted by the guys if we act as if we're in some kind of exclusive sorority," she said.

"Good point. But what's with the clothes? I thought you were protesting the dress code."

"That was Aurora's idea," Lindsay said. "I'm just trying to fit in."

Henry stared at her suspiciously. "Are you sure you're feeling all right?"

"I'm fine. Why?"

"I saw London, I saw France, I saw Lindsay's underpants!" a voice behind her chanted.

Lindsay turned around and found herself looking into Will Dalton's grinning face. *Adapt or Die,* she told herself. She forced herself to smile. "I guess I've learned a thing or two about Randall Hall," she said cheerfully. "Don't sit at the football table, and leave the school traditions to the boys."

Will stared at her dumbfounded. Then a small smile crept over his lips. He looked at Lindsay as if he were seeing her for the first time.

"What's with you, Lindsay?" Henry asked. "You're acting like a total wimp."

Lindsay faced front. "No, I'm not. I'm being a good sport."

"But what you just said sounded like some status-crazed sixth grader sucking up to Chas Randall. You call that being a good sport?"

Lindsay pushed her glasses up her nose. Admittedly, she was turned off by the boys who followed Chas around like groupies after a rock star. But that was different. They were males, members of the Randall Hall majority. She was female, an alien visitor on Planet Boy.

Just then a red-haired boy with a thin nose and a wide smile sat down next to Henry. "Lindsay, this is my friend Evan," Henry said.

"Hey, Lindsay," Evan said. He talked fast, barely pausing to take a breath. "Henry told me he knew you, but I didn't believe him. Did you really meet in the bathroom? Ha! Pretty cool. Hey, how come you're wearing a skirt?"

Lindsay shrugged. "I just wanted to look nice."

"Yeah, but what about the uniform thing? I thought maybe we could all get together and agree to wear regular clothes one day. You know, to protest the uniform rule. Whaddaya say?"

"I don't think so. I decided the uniforms aren't really so bad. Besides, I don't want to buck tradition."

Henry and Evan exchanged baffled glances. "Man, Lindsay, you're really different than I thought at first," Henry said.

Lindsay smiled. Her plan was working! "Thanks," she said.

* * *

When Assembly ended, Lindsay followed Henry and Evan into the quad. To her surprise, she saw that the statue of Charles Bennington Randall was wearing a football uniform. "Hey, that was my idea!" she cried, hurrying over to the statue.

"I guess Chas decided to make it his," Henry said, pointing to the base of the statue. Chas had written his name and the words RANDALL HALL FOREVER in blue chalk on the concrete.

Lindsay could feel her temper boiling like molten lava. *That Chas Randall thinks he's so smart*, she thought furiously. *Well, I'll show him!*

But then she remembered her new motto: Adapt or Die. Chas had been waiting all his life to dress the statue of his great-great-grandfather, she reminded herself. So what if he had embarrassed her and stolen her idea in the process? It wasn't the end of the world.

"That was a nice try yesterday, Tavish," said a voice behind her. Lindsay turned and saw Chas and three of his groupies. Marissa was standing nearby, trying to look as if she belonged. "But I guess it took a boy to dress up the statue right."

Lindsay clenched her fists and forced herself to count to ten. "It looks good," she said at last.

"It took a lot of work to put that varnish on, and even more to remove it," Chas said. "But it was worth it." He chuckled. "You know, those were real nice white undies you had on yesterday, Lindsay. What color are you wearing today?"

Lindsay could feel her ears getting hot. Deep down, she longed to do something that would embarrass Chas as much as he had embarrassed her. Instead, she smiled and said, "Well, I'd better be going. I don't want to be late for class."

She turned to leave. A small crowd of boys had gathered to watch Chas and Lindsay face off. The expressions on their faces made it clear they had expected fireworks but had gotten barely a spark. *Good,* Lindsay thought, walking away.

Henry hurried after her. "I don't get it," he said. "Why did you let Chas put you down like that?"

"Let him have his fun," she replied. "If I don't respond, he'll get bored after a while and go away."

Henry stared at Lindsay and shook his head. "You know, Linds, I was really starting to think you were something special. But now . . . well, I guess I was wrong." He shrugged and walked away.

Lindsay watched him go. Her insides felt twisted, like a swing that had been wound up and released. *Big deal,* she told herself. *So Henry is disappointed to find out I'm not Joan of Arc. Well, so what? Maybe if old Joan had shown a little more grace under pressure, she wouldn't have been burned at the stake.*

"Hi, Lindsay."

She looked up to see Will Dalton walking toward her.

"I think we're going the same way," he said. "Can I carry your books?"

Lindsay couldn't believe her ears. The quarterback of the football team—an eighth grader, no less—wanted to walk her to class!

Suddenly, Lindsay remembered the way Will had humiliated her in the dining hall yesterday. Her neck grew hot and her stomach churned. But then she pushed the feeling aside. After all, that was the old Lindsay whose chair he had hoisted into the air and carried across the cafeteria. *Today he met the new Lindsay,* she reminded herself, *and it's pretty obvious he likes her.*

"Why, thank you, Will," she said, handing over her books. *Adapt or Die,* she told herself. Smiling graciously, she fell into step at his side.

CHAPTER EIGHT

We're going to use the old Flea Flicker play on St. Stephen's," Will said. "The quarterback—that's me—hands off to the running back, who runs up to the line of scrimmage. Then he laterals it to the quarterback—me again—who throws a long bomb for a touchdown."

"Uh-huh," Lindsay muttered, taking a sip of her chocolate milk. It was Monday, the first day of the third week of school, and she was sitting at the football table in the dining hall with Will and his friends.

"You'll get a chance to see the play this Saturday," he said. His eyes took on a faraway look as he added, "I love the first home game of the season. The cheers of the Randall Hall faithful, the smell of grass and Gatorade . . . the sound of crunching bones and spurting blood!" He laughed hysterically and his friends joined in.

Lindsay managed a small chuckle, but her gaze

wandered across the room to the table where Aurora was sitting with Henry and Evan. They were chatting and laughing as they shared a package of cookies. Lindsay wondered what they were talking about.

"But seriously, Lindsay," Will continued, "I was wondering if you'd take some notes for me during the game. I like to keep a record of my plays: who I throw to, how many passes I complete, that kind of thing. Usually my mother does it for me, but I figured, as long as you're going to be there . . ."

"Of course," she replied with her most gracious smile. She hadn't been listening closely to his request, but she knew he expected her to say yes.

"Hey, Will. Hey, Linds."

She glanced up. Fraser was walking by, carrying his lunch tray. Since Lindsay had started hanging out with Will and keeping her mouth shut, her brother had actually been acknowledging her existence in public. "Hey, Frase," she called happily.

Fraser walked on and the conversation shifted back to the St. Stephen's football team and Randall Hall's strategy for beating them. But Lindsay was thinking of other things. So far her Adapt or Die strategy seemed to be working. No one gave her a hard time when she sat beside Will at the football table in the dining hall. His friends always said hi to her, and most importantly, Fraser approved.

But was it worth it? she wondered. Lindsay was sure Will Dalton had to be the most boring person in the entire universe, and his friends weren't much better. *If I hear one more word about football, I think I'll barf,* she thought.

Lindsay glanced around the room, looking for the

other girls. Aurora, Henry, and Evan had left. She had seen them playing Frisbee in the quad during lunch and after school. They always seemed to be laughing, and sometimes Lindsay longed to join them. But she knew Will thought they were "weirdos"—his word for anyone who didn't play or watch football—so she stayed away.

Marissa was sitting at Chas's table. She had spent the last week following him like a shadow, and recently he had actually started talking to her. Elizabeth was in the far corner at an empty table. She was still a loner, and Lindsay thought she seemed a little lonely, too.

So am I, Lindsay admitted. Sometimes she wished she could go back to hanging out with Aurora, Marissa, and Elizabeth, but she didn't know how to break the ice. Besides, she told herself, she'd never be accepted by the boys if she spent all her time with girls.

Will finished eating and stood up to bus his tray. "Come on, Lindsay," he urged. "I want to play a little touch football before the bell rings." Obediently, Lindsay hurried through the last of her meal and jumped up to join him.

On the way out, they passed Ms. Iver. "Lindsay, can I talk to you a moment?" she asked.

"You go ahead, Will," Lindsay said. "I'll be right there."

"I see you've made some new friends," Ms. Iver remarked as Will left.

Lindsay nodded proudly, certain her teacher would be pleased. "I've learned how to fit in."

"If you ask me, you're trying to jam a round peg into a square hole."

"What do you mean?" Lindsay asked.

Ms. Iver didn't answer. "The UAU Committee—that's Uniforms Are Uncool—has fifteen members. I'm a little surprised you aren't one of them."

"What's wrong with tradition?" Lindsay asked defensively.

"Nothing, if the tradition makes as much sense today as it did when it was started." Ms. Iver picked up an abandoned tray and slid it into one of the tray racks that lined the back wall. "The next UAU meeting is a week from today. Aurora and I are going to work on the first draft of a letter to the trustees, requesting that they drop the uniform rule." She leaned against the tray rack and looked at Lindsay. "You're a good writer. Think you might stop by and give us your input?"

Lindsay felt confused. First Ms. Iver had told her to stop sticking out like a sore thumb. Now she was encouraging her to challenge the rules. It didn't make sense. "Will Dalton thinks the UAU committee is weird," she said. "He says football players wear uniforms because it fosters order, unity, and discipline, and students should wear them, too."

"Is that what you think?" Ms. Iver asked.

Lindsay didn't know what to say. What was the right answer? She felt certain that no matter what answer she gave, Ms. Iver would tell her she should think just the opposite. "I don't care if we wear uniforms or dresses or burlap sacks," she blurted out. "I just want to be the person I'm supposed to be."

"Well, that's easy," Ms. Iver said. "Just be yourself."

Lindsay squirmed. Ms. Iver's knowing green eyes seemed to be looking right through her, into the secret place where she kept her deepest feelings. "Will's waiting for me," she said, turning away.

"Go on then."

Lindsay started to walk away.

"Remember, next Monday. Think it over."

But Lindsay didn't want to think. She hurried out of the dining hall and ran to join Will and his friends.

That afternoon Lindsay was sitting on the sofa in the family room, doing her math homework and pigging out on cheddar cheese popcorn. With a satisfied sigh, she wrote down the solution to one of the complicated algebra equations. As she paused to stuff a fistful of popcorn into her mouth, the doorbell rang. Her parents were at work and Fraser was at a tennis lesson, so she had to answer it. She walked to the door and peered through the peephole. It was Fraser's best friends, Mason Fitzpatrick and Phillip Mankowitz.

Chewing frantically, Lindsay opened the door and simultaneously inhaled a piece of popcorn. "Hi," she gasped, breaking into a noisy coughing fit. Bits of moist popcorn flew out of her mouth and splattered against the wall.

"Let me give you a tip, Ms. President," Mason said. "Don't eat popcorn before your inaugural address. It's a real turnoff when you spit at the American people."

"The Secret Service to the rescue!" Phillip cried, pounding her on the back.

Lindsay finally got her cough under control, but not her blushing cheeks. "Fraser isn't here," she said, wiping a smudge of popcorn off the wall with her elbow.

"Too bad," Mason said, jerking his head to flip a lock

of blond hair out of his eyes. "There's a new video arcade at the mall and we're going to check it out."

"Hey, Lindsay, I'm impressed," Phillip remarked. He draped his long, lean body against the door frame. "Only the third week of school and already you've landed an eighth grader."

Lindsay shrugged, half-embarrassed, half-pleased.

"Will Dalton's okay if you're into football," Mason said. "He eats, drinks, and breathes it."

"Let's face it," Phillip said flatly, "the dude's a bore. Still, he *is* a hot quarterback."

"*He* certainly thinks so," Mason quipped. "No offense, Linds," he added.

Lindsay was puzzled. She had assumed Will was one of the most popular boys at school. After all, everyone knew him. He even had his own table in the dining hall. But now it seemed that Mason and Phillip—two very hip eighth graders—thought he was a self-impressed bore.

Lindsay was suddenly aware that Mason was looking her up and down. "You know," he said, "I always thought of you—if I thought of you at all—as Fraser's baby sister. But I gotta say, Linds, you've got hidden depths. I mean, the way you made mincemeat of Chas Randall at that first assembly was awesome."

"And Old Charlie looked outstanding in his girdle," Phillip added. He waggled his eyebrows. "Nice lingerie show, too."

Lindsay felt a wave of prickly heat shoot up the back of her neck. "I was so embarrassed!"

"Who wouldn't be?" Phillip said with a shrug. "But now it's your turn to get back at Chas. Go for it!"

"I don't think Fraser wants me to."

"Oh, *Fraser*," Mason said, dismissing him with a wave of his hand. "What do you expect? He's your brother."

"Sure," Phillip said with a straight face. "Brothers are required to be embarrassed by their sisters. I think they just passed a law about it."

Lindsay laughed.

"All I gotta say is, you made Assembly almost interesting," Phillip concluded. "And believe me, that's not easy." He grabbed Mason's arm. "Let's go. My fingers are itching to touch those brand new video machines."

"So long, Linds," Mason called as they retrieved their bikes from the lawn. "If you can convince the trustees to dump the uniform rule, we'll tear down the statue of Charles Bennington Randall and put up one of you."

"And we'll make Fraser help us!" Phillip added.

Lindsay stood in the doorway, watching them pedal away. She had a brain cramp the size of Pennsylvania. It seemed as if everyone wanted something different from her. Henry, Evan, and Aurora wanted her to speak her mind; and to her surprise, she had now learned that Mason and Phillip did, too. Chas, Will, and their friends, on the other hand, wanted her to keep quiet and play by the rules.

Then there was Fraser. As far as she could figure, he wanted her to drop off the face of the earth and disappear. Short of that, there was nothing she could possibly do that wouldn't embarrass him—at least that's what Mason and Phillip seemed to be saying. *If that's true, why bother?* she told herself. *I might as well just do what I want.*

But what *did* she want? Suddenly, the conversation she'd had with Ms. Iver in the dining hall popped into her head. "I just want to be the person I'm supposed to be," she had said. And Ms. Iver had answered, "That's easy. Just be yourself."

"Just be myself," she said out loud. It was a scary thought. It meant speaking her mind, possibly putting her foot in her mouth, and even risking embarrassing her brother, not to mention herself. Most of all, it meant giving up her dream of being a gracious, charming, superachieving Tavish. It meant not being perfect.

Suddenly, the phone rang, jarring Lindsay from her thoughts. She ran back into the family room and answered it. "Tavish residence."

"Lindsay, is that you? This is Marissa."

Lindsay's heart soared, and that surprised her. She hadn't realized until now just how much she missed talking to the other girls. "Hi," she said eagerly. "How are you?"

"Fine. Terrific. Fantastic! Chas asked me out this Saturday after the football game. We're going to a movie at the mall."

Marissa's mad passion for Chas Randall baffled Lindsay, but she didn't want to rain on her friend's parade. "Good for you," she said.

"I knew you'd understand. I've seen you with Will Dalton. Isn't love wonderful?"

"I'm not sure I'd call my feelings for Will *love* exactly," Lindsay began, but Marissa didn't seem to hear her.

"I'm so nervous about Saturday," she continued breathlessly. "That's why I'm calling. I was going to ask you to meet me at the mall before Chas shows up—you know, for moral support. But I have an even better idea. We can double date! You and Will, and me and Chas. What do you think?"

Lindsay couldn't think of anything she would like less than to spend an afternoon with Will Dalton and Chas Randall. On the other hand, making friends with Chas would be another big step into the Randall Hall "in" crowd. And that meant fitting in big time. Besides, she didn't want to disappoint Marissa. She paused, uncertain how to answer.

Then she remembered Ms. Iver's words. "Just be yourself." *Okay, what do I really want?* she asked herself. The answer came to her almost immediately. She wanted to make up with Aurora, Marissa, and Elizabeth. She didn't want to double date with Will and Chas.

"Will has a football game that morning," Lindsay said. "He'll be too tired to go on a date in the afternoon. But maybe you could ask Aurora and Henry."

"Aurora? Ha! I wouldn't ask her for a glass of water if my head were on fire!"

"Oh, come on, Marissa. I think we should all make up. I miss the girls, don't you?"

"I miss *you*. Come on, Lindsay, can't you at least meet me at the mall before my date? Please? I just need someone to talk to."

Lindsay was about to answer when suddenly she had an idea. It was fantastic, and best of all, it was so *Lindsay*. "Sure, Marissa, I'd be happy to meet you before your date," she said. "What time is the movie?"

Marissa squealed with delight. "Three o'clock. Oh,

Lindsay, I can't decide what to wear. Maybe my pink dress with the puffy sleeves? No, too dressy. How about jeans and a suede jacket? Oh, I just realized something. This will be my first glimpse of Chas in something other than his school uniform!"

Marissa babbled on, but Lindsay's mind was on other things. If her plan worked, Aurora, Marissa, Elizabeth, and she would be Randy's Raiders once again. If it backfired, the Middleford Mall would probably witness the sixth-grade version of World War III.

CHAPTER NINE

*L*indsay, over here!"

Lindsay looked across the Middleford Mall, past the throngs of Saturday shoppers, screaming toddlers, and cruising teenagers to the fountain in the middle of the food court. Marissa was sitting on the edge of it, dangling her hand in the water. She was wearing tight black jeans, a turquoise silk blouse, and makeup, and her eyes were shining with eager anticipation.

Lindsay waved and hurried toward her, checking her watch as she went. Two-thirty exactly. So far everything was going according to plan. She had told each girl to meet her at the mall at two-thirty, never mentioning that the others would also be there. Her hope was that the element of surprise would shock everyone out of their anger and convince them to make up.

"You look gorgeous!" Lindsay exclaimed, joining

91

Marissa on the edge of the fountain.

"Oh, Lindsay, I'm so excited, I think I'm going to explode."

"Relax. It's just Chas. You see him practically every day."

"But this is different. It's our first date."

"What movie are you going to see?" Lindsay asked.

"He didn't say." She sighed and let her fingers glide through the water. "I hope it's something romantic."

"Hey, what's *she* doing here?" an accusing voice demanded.

Lindsay and Marissa looked up to see Aurora staring down at them suspiciously. She was wearing black bicycle shorts, a baggy, red, long-sleeved T-shirt, and green hightops. A skateboard was tucked under one arm.

"Hi, Aurora," Lindsay began cheerfully, "I asked all of you to—"

"Lindsay said she'd meet me here before my date with Chas," Marissa broke in. "What's your excuse?"

"Lindsay called me up yesterday and said she wanted to talk to me," Aurora shot back. "She told me to meet her here for lunch."

"What's going on?" a small voice asked.

Lindsay, Marissa, and Aurora turned. Elizabeth was standing a few feet away, looking like a young deer that had just come upon a pack of coyotes. She was wearing faded jeans and a white blouse, and her black hair hung free.

"Hi, Elizabeth," Lindsay said with a reassuring smile. "Come on over."

"I thought you wanted to make up," she said.

"I do," Lindsay announced. "I want us all to make up."

A look of understanding crossed Elizabeth's face. "You tricked me," she said angrily.

"Yeah," Marissa said, turning to Lindsay. "You promised to spend time with me before my date. I'm not sharing you with *them*."

"Well, that's a typical Marissa line if ever I've heard one," Aurora said. "Look at *me*. Pay attention to *me*." She rolled her eyes. "Give it a rest, why don't you?"

"Hey, you guys, come on," Lindsay broke in. "Let's be friends."

"You don't want to be friends with me," Elizabeth said. "None of you does. I'm not part of your crowd."

"How would you know?" Marissa asked. "You always have your nose stuck so far in the air, you can't see us."

"Look who's talking," Elizabeth snapped. "You're so stuck up, you probably have sunburned nostrils!"

Lindsay groaned. Things were turning out all wrong. Her clever plan was about to crash and burn. *I have to turn things around, and fast,* she told herself. *But how?*

"I knew I should have paid closer attention to my horoscope," Aurora was saying with disgust. "It said today I would meet three fools by the water and be washed clean."

Lindsay looked up. Aurora's words gave her an idea. If it worked, it just might save the day. If it backfired, she'd probably be banned from the Middleford Mall for the rest of her life.

"Watch out, fools," Lindsay exclaimed, "it's time to be washed clean!" With that, she dipped her fingers into the fountain and flung a handful of water at Aurora, Marissa, and

Elizabeth. It splashed into their faces and sprayed their hair.

The girls froze, shocked into silence. Rivulets of water ran down their noses and dripped onto their shirts. Lindsay grinned and reached into the fountain for another handful.

"Don't you dare!" Aurora warned.

"Try and stop me," Lindsay replied with a smile.

Aurora dropped her skateboard and lunged at Lindsay's arm. Lindsay pulled away and Aurora's own arm plunged into the fountain instead. When she pulled it out, the sleeve of her T-shirt was dripping wet.

Aurora stared at her soggy sleeve. She looked as if she didn't know whether to laugh or go ballistic. She glanced at Lindsay, then her eyes widened with sudden inspiration. With a mischievous smile on her face, she turned and flung her wet arm at Marissa.

Beads of water sprayed across Marissa's face. She gasped and reached up to touch her cheek. "You smeared my makeup!" she wailed. With her eyes flashing, she dipped her hand into the fountain and splashed water at Aurora. But Aurora jumped aside and the water landed on Elizabeth's jeans instead.

Elizabeth gasped, then turned to Marissa. Her eyes narrowed.

"It's not my fault," Marissa said quickly. "I was aiming for Aurora."

"Lindsay's the one who started the whole thing," Aurora pointed out. An evil smile played on her lips. "I say we dunk her."

"Whoa!" Lindsay cried, backing up as Aurora advanced menacingly toward her. "Let's not get carried—"

But before she could say another word, Aurora, Marissa, and Elizabeth pounced on her. They forced her to her knees at the edge of the fountain and dunked her entire head in the water.

Lindsay came up, sputtering and giggling. The other girls took one look at her wet face, crooked glasses, and dripping hair and burst out laughing.

"There now, that's more like it," Lindsay said, grinning through her limp hair. "I knew if we had a common goal, we'd all learn to work together."

Everyone cracked up. "Lindsay, you're a drip!" Marissa giggled, which made them laugh even harder.

Lindsay wrung her hair out over the fountain. The girls broke into another giggling fit.

"Randy's Raiders are back!" Aurora proclaimed. She tried to wipe the water off Lindsay's glasses with her sleeve, forgetting that her T-shirt was still wet. The glass turned into a smeary mess, and the girls laughed until they were too weak to move.

Then suddenly, Elizabeth fell silent. "Uh-oh!" she breathed. "Look!"

Still giggling, Lindsay turned. A crowd had formed to watch their antics. Even the employees of Shanghai Express and Creative Croissants had paused to stare at them. But the real news was the two mall security guards who were striding purposefully out of Sears. Thanks to the crowds the guards hadn't caught sight of the girls yet, but there was no doubt in Lindsay's mind that they were heading their way.

"Let's get out of here!" Aurora cried, scooping up her skateboard.

"But where will we go?" Elizabeth asked.

"The ladies' room," Marissa said. "Come on."

The girls started walking, slowly at first, and then faster. Lindsay stayed behind long enough to grab a few napkins from an empty table and wipe the water from the floor. Then she ran after the girls as they hurried into the ladies' room.

"I guess we were fated to be friends," Elizabeth said, shaking her head in amazement as the door closed behind them.

"You sound like Aurora," Marissa said. "I suppose you consulted a psychic about this."

Elizabeth giggled. "Not exactly. But I do read my horoscope every day."

"Way to go, sister," Aurora said, slapping palms with Elizabeth.

Marissa turned to the mirror and her face fell. "My makeup is a disaster. And my hair! I can't meet Chas looking like this!"

"Don't be silly," Lindsay said. "You look fabulous."

"My parents would never let me wear makeup like that," Elizabeth said wistfully. "They have a fit if I even use lip gloss."

"My father thinks girls should look pretty," Marissa said with a shrug.

"What about your mother?" Aurora asked.

"She died when I was three," Marissa answered. "She was really beautiful. Both my sisters look just like her."

"Who do you look like?" Lindsay asked.

Marissa frowned into the mirror. "No one. I'm the ugly duckling of the family."

"Oh, get real!" Aurora exclaimed with a laugh.

But Marissa wasn't laughing. For the first time since Lindsay had met her, she looked vulnerable and a little sad. "It's almost time to meet Chas," Lindsay said, gently touching her friend's shoulder. "You don't want to be late."

Marissa gasped and snapped into action. She dried her hair with paper towels, then bent at the waist and fluffed up her curls. Then she opened her purse and set about reapplying her makeup: lipstick, blusher, and mascara. When she was finished, she looked like a model straight off the cover of a magazine.

"What are you three going to do while I'm at the movie?" she asked, popping a breath mint into her mouth.

"Eat," Aurora said with feeling. She turned to Lindsay. "We were supposed to be meeting for lunch, remember?"

"There's a new Mexican restaurant next to Macy's," Lindsay replied. "Do you want to try it?"

"I haven't had Mexican since I left California, and I've been totally craving it," Aurora said eagerly. "Like last night I actually dreamed I was floating on a tortilla in an ocean of guacamole. I mean, I'm so desperate, I've been buying microwaved burritos at the 7-Eleven!"

"I'm sick of Mexican," Elizabeth protested. "I eat it all the time. Besides, this place serves gringo Mexican—the kind of stuff that appeals to Mr. and Mrs. Middle America. It won't be half as good as what you're used to eating in California."

"I don't care," Aurora replied. "If it's got tortilla chips and salsa I'll be happy."

"But—"

"Oh, come on, Elizabeth," Lindsay asked. "You can introduce me to some new dishes. The only Mexican food I've ever eaten is nachos."

"Yeah, but—"

"You can argue about this later," Marissa said, turning from the mirror. "Chas is waiting for me."

They left the ladies' room and walked through the mall. Lindsay searched the crowds for security guards, but there were none in sight. "Do you want us to meet you after the movie?" she asked.

"Chas might want to walk me home," Marissa replied with a coy smile. "But why don't you stop by the theater entrance around four-thirty?"

Lindsay rolled her eyes. The vulnerable, uncertain Marissa had disappeared and the old Marissa was back—flirtatious and full of herself. With a wave and a flip of her curls, she headed off toward the multiplex cinemas at the north end of the mall.

The Mexican restaurant was up ahead. The sign said El Mar Azul. "What does it mean?" Lindsay asked.

"The Blue Sea," Elizabeth said. "Yuck, it's probably a fish restaurant. Let's go to McDonald's."

"No way," Aurora cried. "I can smell the cilantro and chilies. Come on!" She grabbed Lindsay and Elizabeth by the arm and practically dragged them into the restaurant.

They were met at the door by the hostess, a plump, middle-aged woman with dark hair pulled back into a bun and a warm, welcoming face. Her eyes lit up when she saw them. *"Hola, mi hija,"* she exclaimed, hurrying up and patting Elizabeth's cheek. *"Presentame a tus amigas."*

"What did she say?" Aurora asked.

"She asked if we wanted smoking or nonsmoking," Elizabeth said. She turned to the hostess and spoke in an angry murmur. "*Mama, por favor, no me pongas en rediculo.*"

"Did you say 'Mama'?" Lindsay asked with surprise.

"My English not so good," the hostess said haltingly in a thick Mexican accent. "I want to say *bienvenido* to the school friends of my daughter. What is the word? Welcome!"

"You mean, Elizabeth is your daughter?" Lindsay asked in astonishment.

"*Sí.* I mean, yes." She bustled the girls into the restaurant and led them to an empty table by the window. "Sit, please. Elizabeth tells me many good things about her new friends. I make something *especial* for you." With that she hurried away.

"Okay, now you know," Elizabeth said defensively. "My parents aren't big shots like yours. We aren't rich and famous."

"My parents aren't big shots," Lindsay protested.

Elizabeth laughed disdainfully. "My family moved to this country from Mexico five years ago. Until last summer we lived with my aunt in West Philadelphia. Now we live in Middleford, in a tiny apartment by the railroad tracks. I'm going to Randall Hall on a full scholarship."

"So?" Aurora said with a shrug.

"I don't belong in your world. Last year I went to an all-girls' Catholic school run by nuns!" She paused and stared down at her hands. "I'm not stuck-up like you think," she whispered. "I just keep my mouth closed so I won't say anything stupid."

"Oh, Elizabeth," Lindsay said sympathetically, reaching out to touch her hand, "you don't have to be shy around us. We're friends, right?"

"But it's not the same for me," she insisted. "Remember when I phoned you to say I didn't have a blue blazer? You couldn't understand why I didn't just go to a thrift shop and buy one. But I had to work here at the restaurant all afternoon and most of the evening. Besides, my mother would never let me spend money on such foolishness."

Just then Mrs. Lopez reappeared with a big plate of steaming, delicious-smelling pastries. "*Sopapillas*," she announced, setting them down on the table. "You eat with honey." Behind her came a handsome, middle-aged man with a dark mustache, followed by two little girls. "My husband bring s*opa de fideo*—special Mexican soup," she said. "Ah, and these are Elizabeth's sisters, Claudia *y* Felicia."

"Hi," Lindsay and Aurora said together. The girls giggled and hid behind Mrs. Lopez's skirt.

"Eat, eat," Mr. Lopez urged.

Eagerly, Lindsay and Aurora dug in. Mr. and Mrs. Lopez waited anxiously for their reactions.

"Oh, wow!" Lindsay exclaimed as the warm *sopapilla* melted in her mouth.

"Totally cosmic!" Aurora cried. "I'm having an out-of-body experience!"

Mr. and Mrs. Lopez looked at Elizabeth uncertainly.

"They like it," Elizabeth explained.

"Ah, *bueno!*" Mrs. Lopez said. "Now, you wait. I bring you my famous tamales." She and her husband returned to the kitchen.

"Your parents are really nice, Elizabeth," Lindsay said.

"Yeah," Aurora agreed between sips of soup. "And imagine having homemade Mexican food whenever you want. Too cool!"

"But you must have really fancy food at your house," Elizabeth said. "Real gourmet stuff."

"Are you kidding?" Aurora laughed. "My mother is on an eternal diet. All we have in our refrigerator is yogurt and frozen dinners."

"My parents don't get home until seven or eight o'clock," Lindsay said. "Fraser and I usually end up making something for ourselves—macaroni and cheese or a hamburger."

Elizabeth looked stunned. She reached for a *sopapilla* and took a bite. "*Delicioso*," she said thoughtfully.

At that moment the door of the restaurant flew open and Marissa rushed in. Her eyes were red, her nose was running, and her cheeks were stained with tears. When she saw the girls, she ran to their table and threw herself into an empty chair.

"Marissa, what happened?" Lindsay asked.

Marissa looked at Lindsay and burst into noisy sobs. "I hate Chas Randall!" she wailed. "I hate him, I hate him, I hate him!"

CHAPTER TEN

W hat happened?" Aurora asked. "Didn't he show up?"

"He showed, but he wasn't alone," Marissa said between sniffles. "He had four of his friends with him. He acted real surprised to see me, too."

"What a creep!" Elizabeth exclaimed. "And after he'd asked you on a date and everything."

"Well, he never exactly called it a date," Marissa admitted sheepishly. "But last Monday he told me he was going to the movies this afternoon and I said, 'Me, too,' and he said, 'See you there.' So I figured—well, I thought at least he'd be happy to see me."

"So what happened?" Lindsay asked.

"He and the guys hung around outside the multiplex talking for a while. I told myself it was going to be okay, that at least I'd be able to sit next to him during the movie.

But then Alex Lithgow said, 'Have you seen the new video arcade they opened next to the bookstore?' and Chas said, 'No, is it any good?' and Alex said, 'It's a killer,' and so they all decided to forget the movie and go to the arcade."

"And they didn't ask you along?" Aurora wanted to know.

"No," Marissa said, her voice cracking. "Chas just turned to me and said, 'So long, Marissa. Enjoy the movie.' And then he left." She burst out crying again. "Oh, I hate him, I hate him, I hate him!"

Just then Mrs. Lopez arrived with the tamales. "Ah, another friend. Welcome!" Then she noticed Marissa's tears. "My, my, what is wrong, *niña?*"

"Boy trouble," Aurora explained.

"*Pobrecita*. Poor thing! Have a *sopapilla*," she said, offering the plate to Marissa. "The sweetness will take away the bitter memory."

Marissa took a bite and smiled through her tears. "They're good," she said.

After Mrs. Lopez left, Elizabeth showed the girls how to eat the tamales. "They're cooked in corn husks," she explained, unwrapping one. "Inside is *masa*—cornmeal dough—plus minced pork and vegetables."

"Elizabeth's parents own this restaurant," Lindsay told Marissa. She decided to wait until she and Marissa were alone to reveal the other things she had learned about Elizabeth that afternoon.

"Your mom is nice," Marissa said, sniffling as she took a bite of tamale.

Elizabeth grinned shyly. "Thanks."

"Chas looked so cute," Marissa went on. "He was

wearing faded jeans and a Swarthmore College sweat shirt, and his hair was all windblown." She sighed dejectedly.

Lindsay shook her head in disbelief. Marissa might be temporarily mad at Chas, but it was obvious she still had a massive crush on him. She decided to change the subject. "Elizabeth went to parochial school before she came to Randall Hall. How about you, Marissa?"

"Public school," she answered, sipping her soup. "Middleford Elementary. But then my dad's business made a lot of money, so he built a big house and sent all of us to private school. What about you?"

"Middleford Country Day School," Lindsay replied, naming the area's most prestigious private elementary school. "It's kind of like Randall Hall, only coed."

"Did Fraser go there, too?" Elizabeth asked.

Lindsay shook her head. "My parents sent him to Franklin Boys Academy in Philadelphia because it has a better tennis program. How about you, Aurora?"

"Back in California I went to the Topanga Canyon Free School. It's a progressive school, real alternative. It was started by some hippie friends of my dad back in the sixties. But when my parents got divorced and my mom moved here, she decided to turn herself—and me—into preppies."

"I don't think it's working," Elizabeth remarked.

"Good," Aurora replied, flipping her blond hair behind her shoulder as she stuffed a honey-drenched *sopapilla* into her mouth.

"Hey, does anyone know what Founder's Day is?" Marissa asked suddenly.

"Sure," Lindsay answered. "It's the anniversary of the

day Randall Hall School was founded, September thirtieth, 1902."

"September thirtieth?" Aurora repeated. "That's next Saturday."

"Didn't you read the handout they gave us in Assembly last week?" Elizabeth asked. "On Founder's Day the school is having an open house. Our families are invited." She gazed down at her plate. "I tried to talk my parents out of coming, but they won't hear of it."

"What's the problem?" Marissa asked. "Everyone's parents will be there."

"Yes, but my parents don't understand English very well, and I have to translate everything for them. Besides, you saw how friendly they are to everyone. My father will probably slap Mr. Bertozzi on the back, and my mother will hug him."

"Excellent!" Aurora laughed. "He needs to loosen up a little." The girls giggled.

"Chas was telling the guys that on Founder's Day it's a tradition for a group of sixth graders to sneak a pig into the library," Marissa said.

"A pig?" Elizabeth asked incredulously. "Why?"

"Because the first headmaster's name was Mr. Piggle," she explained. "It started out as a joke on him, but even after he retired, the sixth graders kept up the tradition. Chas says that every year the boys who pull it off become class heroes."

"And let me guess," Aurora said. "This year it's going to be him."

Marissa nodded. "But Chas plans to outdo every sixth-grade class that came before him. He said that since the school teams are called the Randall Hall Stallions, he wants to sneak a stallion into the library. Only, actually, he'll use a pony, because they're smaller and easier to handle and his cousin has one."

As Marissa spoke, Lindsay's brain switched into high gear. She thought about the last traditional stunt she and the girls had tried to pull off—dressing the statue of old Charlie—and she remembered how Chas had humiliated her in front of the entire school. On top of that, he had stolen her idea and grabbed all the glory for himself. Then she remembered what Phillip Mankowitz had said to her last week: "Now it's your turn to get back at Chas. Go for it!"

A smile played on Lindsay's lips. If only she could find a way to one-up Chas this time! But the smile disappeared as her mind was bombarded with reasons why she shouldn't try: Fraser wouldn't approve. Will Dalton and his friends would call her a weirdo. Chas might find a way to make her look ridiculous, just like last time. Besides, considering Lindsay's talent for putting her foot in her mouth, there was a good chance she would end up getting in trouble, making a fool of herself, and generally disgracing the Tavish name.

Then Lindsay remembered Ms. Iver's words: "Just be yourself." Her teacher's advice had worked once already—when Lindsay had decided to bring all the girls together at the mall. *That's right,* Lindsay told herself. *I followed my heart and won my friends back. Why shouldn't I follow my heart again?*

Before she could change her mind, she opened her mouth and blurted out, "Chas isn't going to put a pony in the library. *We* are."

"What?" Elizabeth gasped.

"Oh, no," Marissa groaned. "Is this going to be another one of your no-brainer stunts, like wearing Randall Hall uniforms or dressing the statue of Charles Bennington Randall?"

"No, this is going to be better," Lindsay said firmly. "Besides, what's the problem? I should think if anyone wanted to one-up Chas Randall, it would be you."

"That's right," Aurora pointed out. "In the last fifteen minutes we've heard you say you hate his guts at least six times."

"Besides, this isn't just about getting back at Chas," Lindsay added. "It's about making a name for ourselves at Randall Hall, and proving that school traditions aren't for boys only."

"So what's the plan?" Elizabeth asked skeptically.

"The plan?" Lindsay wrinkled her brow. "Well, uh, I haven't quite figured that out yet. I guess we need to beat Chas to the library and maybe put our own pony in there instead."

"Oh, sure," Marissa scoffed. "And where are we going to get our hands on a pony?"

"Well . . . uh . . ." Lindsay faltered.

"Forget the pony," Aurora broke in. "If we want to put a Randall Hall Stallion in the library, I say go for the real thing."

"Oh, now it's a stallion," Marissa said disdainfully. "Where are we going to find one of those?"

"At my house," Aurora said. "His name is Mel. Mel Gibson gave him to my father after they filmed a movie together. My mother won him in the divorce settlement."

"*Ahora, niñas,* are you ready for dessert?"

The girls looked up to see Mr. and Mrs. Lopez standing over them, holding four dishes.

"Flan," Mrs. Lopez said. "Custard with . . . what is it, *mi hija?*"

"Caramelized sugar on top," Elizabeth explained.

Mr. and Mrs. Lopez put down the dishes and the girls dug in.

"Yum!" Lindsay exclaimed. "It melts in your mouth!" Aurora and Marissa nodded happily.

Satisfied, Mr. and Mrs. Lopez hurried away to wait on another table.

"Okay, are we agreed?" Lindsay asked between bites of flan. "We're going to sneak Aurora's horse into the library the night before Founder's Day, right?"

"But how?" Elizabeth insisted.

"We'll work out the details later," Aurora said. She held up a spoonful of flan. "Here's to Randy's Raiders, and to Mel—the stallion that's going to make Chas Randall the laughingstock of the school and *us* the new heroes!"

Elizabeth paused, then hesitantly clinked her spoon against Aurora's.

Marissa bit her lip, thinking it over. "Oh, well," she said at last. "Flirting with Chas hasn't worked. Maybe it's time to play hard to get." She shrugged and clinked spoons.

Now it was Lindsay's turn. Aurora, Marissa, and Elizabeth were gazing expectantly at her. She knew they were counting on her to come up with a plan that was daring, bold, clever, and, most of all, foolproof. But how?

And then she had a thought. This was Fraser's third

year at Randall Hall. He had to have some idea of how a group of sixth graders would sneak a horse—or at least a pig—into the library. Maybe she could worm the information out of him without actually letting on that she was planning to pull off the stunt herself. At least it was worth a try.

"To Randy's Raiders!" she exclaimed, trying to sound more confident than she felt. She clinked her spoon with so much enthusiasm, she knocked everyone's flan onto the table. The girls groaned. Lindsay looked down at the quivering pile of custard. *If this is any indication of how things are going to turn out,* she thought nervously, *I'm in a lot of trouble.*

When Lindsay got home from the mall that afternoon, she found her mother in the living room, looking over a set of blueprints. "The plans for the new hospital wing," she said, motioning Lindsay to join her. "What do you think?"

She reached under the blueprints and pulled out a sketch of the building's exterior. It was a graceful brick-and-wood structure with lots of windows and skylights. "It's beautiful," Lindsay said. "Not drab and dreary like most hospitals."

Her mother smiled, and Lindsay felt as if the sun was shining just for her. "That was my intention," she said. "It's a very innovative design, really. Most of the board was pushing for a traditional structure designed by a New Jersey firm, but I just fell in love with this plan by a firm from Japan. Luckily, I did a little research and came up with some facts and figures that convinced them."

"Those guys on the board probably never knew what hit them," Lindsay said.

Her mother laughed. "Well, I *was* rather persuasive—in an understated way, of course."

"I was pretty persuasive this afternoon, too," Lindsay said. "The girls at school—well, they'd had sort of a falling out. But I convinced them to make up and be friends."

"Why, Lindsay, I'm proud of you," her mother said, looking her over with a combination of surprise and satisfaction. "You're really maturing."

Lindsay wondered if her mother would be as proud if she knew that her daughter's method of persuasion had involved splashing her friends with water and allowing herself to be dunked in the mall fountain!

I guess I'll never have the Tavish charm, she thought glumly. Still, she reminded herself, she had gotten results, and wasn't that what counted? Now if she could just do as well on Founder's Day. . . .

Suddenly, a dull *ponk ponk* sound reverberated through the floor. Lindsay knew it was Fraser, practicing his tennis strokes against the basement wall. It was a method he had been using ever since he learned that a big tennis star had practiced that way when he was a kid.

Leaving her mother to her blueprints, Lindsay hurried down to the basement. She found Fraser blasting backhand shots off the concrete wall beside the washer and dryer. "Hi, Fraser!" she called.

Startled, Fraser's stroke went wild. The ball bounced off the wall and shot directly back at him. He ducked just in time. "Thanks, Linds," he said irritably. "I needed a second part in my hair."

"Sorry," Lindsay said with her most charming smile. "Uh, can I ask you a question?"

"If you ask it fast and loud," he replied, returning to his backstroke. The balls hit the wall with a loud *whap!*

"You know that tradition about putting a pig in the library on Founder's Day?" Lindsay shouted. "Pretty funny, huh?"

"Yeah. So?"

"So . . . uh, Will Dalton and I have a bet going. I say the kids steal a key and take the pig in through the front door. Will says they jimmy open a window and climb in. What do you think?"

Fraser stopped hitting and turned to stare at her. "Don't do it."

"Don't do what?"

"You know what I mean. I'm telling you, leave the pig stunt to the sixth-grade boys."

Lindsay's temper began to simmer. "Why?" she asked. "Don't you think a girl can pull it off?"

"It's not that. I just don't want you making a fool of yourself like last time. You'll just embarrass yourself—and me."

"Is that all you care about?" Lindsay demanded. "Don't you ever want to let yourself go? I mean, sometimes I just want to stand on the highest mountaintop and scream, 'Hey, world, look at me!'"

"Yeah, and that's exactly what you've been doing ever since you came to Randy Hall," Fraser snapped. He sighed and paused to even up the strings on his racket. "Look, everything has been cool since you started hanging out with Will Dalton and his friends. Why do you want to rock the boat?"

Lindsay started to answer, but Fraser cut her off. "I mean, look at it this way, Linds," he said. "Why do you need to be the first woman president, anyway? What's wrong with being the First Lady?"

Lindsay's temper shot to a full boil. She opened her mouth, ready to tell Fraser the truth—that Will Dalton left her cold, that she and the girls were going to put a stallion in the library, with or without his help, *and* that her first act as president of the United States was going to be to punch him in the nose.

But then she remembered her mother. She wouldn't blurt out a secret plan just because a man had criticized her. *She* would find a way to turn the situation to her advantage.

Lindsay took a deep breath, turned down the burner under her temper, and said sweetly, "You know, you're right, Fraser."

"I am?" he asked with surprise.

She nodded. "And believe me, I'm not planning any more wild stunts. I just want to win the bet. So won't you tell me what you know about sneaking a pig into the library? Please?"

Fraser gazed at her thoughtfully. She wasn't sure if he believed her or not. Then slowly his eyes narrowed and he smiled slightly. "Okay," he said, tossing his tennis racket onto the washing machine, "you win. I'll tell you everything you need to know."

*S*o according to Fraser," Lindsay explained, "the janitors unlock all the buildings to clean them, and they don't lock them again until they're ready to leave for the night."

"But when is that?" Elizabeth asked.

"Fraser said he's not sure what time they clean the library, but he's pretty sure they lock up around seven-thirty or eight."

It was Sunday afternoon and the girls were at Aurora's house, making plans. Aurora and her mother lived in a Colonial-era stone farmhouse surrounded by five acres of land. The house was decorated with expensive antiques— all except Aurora's room, which was painted hot pink and filled with crystals, electric guitars, a drum set, and back issues of surfing and skateboarding magazines.

Aurora stretched out on her water bed. It rocked

gently. "Then the trick is to sneak into the library with the pig—or in this case, with Mel—*after* the janitors have finished cleaning but *before* they've locked all the buildings and left for the night."

Lindsay nodded. "Then we tie the horse to one of the tables and put a plastic sheet under him," she continued. "You know, so he doesn't mess on the carpet."

"It better be a large plastic sheet," Elizabeth said. "Horses make a *big* mess."

The girls giggled. "It sounds as if we have to get Mel to Randy Hall right after dinner on Friday night," Marissa said. "But how?"

Aurora pondered for a moment. "I need some cookies to help me think," she said, reaching behind her pillow and pulling out a package of chocolate cookies. She took one and passed the bag around.

"None for me, thanks," Marissa said. "I'm on a diet."

"You sound like my mother," Aurora said. A door opened downstairs. "There she is now, back from her riding lesson."

"With Mel?" Elizabeth asked.

Aurora nodded and stuffed the package of cookies back behind her pillow. A moment later her mother appeared at the bedroom door. She was a tall woman, thin as a model, with long blond hair like her daughter's and perfect skin. She was wearing jodhpurs, high leather boots, a tweed jacket, and a black velvet riding cap. Lindsay thought she looked more like a member of the Royal Family than the ex-wife of a Hollywood actor.

"So these are the Randall Hall girls," she said with a smile. "I'm delighted to meet you." She glanced at Aurora and suddenly frowned. "Are those cookie crumbs at the corner of your mouth, young lady?"

"Mo-ther," Aurora groaned.

"I've told you a million times, you take after your father when it comes to food. He just has to look at a jelly doughnut and he gains five pounds."

"Is Mel in his stable?" Aurora asked, ignoring her.

"Yes. Now don't forget, I'm having some women over for tea at four and I want you to help me pour."

"Come on, Mom, I want to go skateboarding this afternoon."

"Not today. And wear something nice—not those bicycle shorts." She glanced at the girls. "It's been a pleasure," she said.

"Your mother is so pretty!" Marissa breathed as Mrs. Barclay walked away.

Elizabeth nodded. "She looks more like your big sister than your mother."

Aurora shrugged. "They can perform miracles with plastic surgery these days. Come on, let's ride Mel."

The girls went downstairs and outside. The back yard was vast. There was a huge expanse of lush grass, a formal garden, and a grape arbor. A stone path led to the stables and riding ring.

"This place is like something out of a TV show," Elizabeth said with awe.

"It's my mom's latest obsession," Aurora answered, unimpressed. "She likes to reinvent herself every couple of years. Back in L.A. she went through her Beverly Hills shopaholic phase, followed by her New Age fitness-health food phase. In this incarnation, she's the perfect country gentlewoman." She rolled her eyes. "She's a better actor than my father."

As they neared the stables, a chicken fluttered out of the bushes and walked across the path, scratching and pecking at the ground. Marissa let out a gasp and froze until the chicken disappeared into the foliage. "This place is a regular zoo," she said with horror.

"I told you my mother was obsessed," Aurora replied. "She's got chickens, peacocks, a few sheep, even a pig. The gardeners take care of them. She just walks around and looks at them once in a while."

Lindsay laughed. Aurora was a real character, but it seemed her mother was even wackier. She wondered if Mr. Barclay was equally goofy, but she didn't think it was polite to ask.

Aurora led the girls into the stables. Mel was in his stall, chomping on a pile of hay. Elizabeth stopped and let out a gasp. "He's beautiful!" she cried.

Lindsay had to agree. Mel's legs were long, his chestnut coat was sleek and shiny, and his big, brown eyes were warm and intelligent. As the girls approached, he left the hay and turned to greet them.

Aurora patted the horse's muscular neck. Hesitantly, Lindsay reached up and did the same. She liked horses, but she hadn't spent much time around them. To tell the truth, they made her a little nervous.

Suddenly, Mel let out a loud snort. Lindsay gasped and leaped backward. "What did I do?"

"Nothing," Aurora laughed. "Relax. He won't hurt you."

Cautiously, Lindsay inched forward and patted Mel again. He fixed one huge brown eye on her. She looked back and smiled. "Hi, Mel. Can you introduce me to Mel Gibson?" The girls giggled.

Elizabeth reached into her pocket and pulled out a sugar cube. She fed it to Mel and rubbed his face. The horse responded by nuzzling her shoulder.

"He likes you," Aurora said. "Do you ride?"

"Not around here," Elizabeth replied. "But one of my uncles owns a ranch in Mexico. When we visit, he takes us riding in the mountains."

"What about you?" Aurora asked, turning to Marissa. She was standing a few feet away with a stricken look on her face. "Don't you want to pet him?"

"He's . . . he's so big," Marissa gasped, wide-eyed.

"I take it you've never been around horses before." Aurora chuckled.

Marissa shook her head and swallowed hard.

"Oh, he's a pussycat," Aurora said. "Come on, let's take him for a ride." She found Mel's bridle, dragged a ladder from the corner of the stable, climbed up, and fitted the bridle into place.

"What about the saddle?" Elizabeth asked.

"Too much trouble," Aurora answered. "We're just going to take him around the pen." She tossed a blanket over Mel's back and led him into the ring. The girls followed. "Who wants to go first?"

"You're not getting me up on that creature," Marissa said firmly.

Aurora rolled her eyes. "Come on, Lindsay, let's you and I ride together. Then Elizabeth can have a turn."

"Okay," Lindsay said, trying to hide her nervousness. She hadn't been on a horse since her parents took her on

117

the pony ride at Middleford County Park when she was three years old. Unfortunately, her pony had decided to sit down in the middle of the ride, and Lindsay had dissolved into hysterical tears. It had taken a double-decker chocolate ice cream cone to finally calm her down.

Aurora led Mel to the edge of the ring, climbed onto the fence, and scrambled easily onto his back. Lindsay felt like asking Aurora if she had any chocolate ice cream back at the house. Instead, she climbed the fence and jumped on behind Aurora.

"Yikes!" she cried breathlessly, throwing her arms around Aurora's waist. "We must be ten feet off the ground!"

"Loosen your grip," Aurora gasped, prying Lindsay's fingers from her waist. "You're squeezing me so tight, I'm going to hurl!"

Lindsay released her grip ever so slightly. Aurora shook Mel's reins and the horse began to walk briskly around the ring. Slowly, Lindsay began to relax. "Hey, this is fun!" she exclaimed.

Elizabeth and Marissa sat on the fence, watching Aurora and Lindsay circle the ring. "So what's the plan?" Marissa asked, eying Mel warily as he passed her. "How do we get the horse to school and into the library?"

"I've figured out the first part," Aurora announced. "I'm going to ride him to Randy Hall."

"Can you do that?" Elizabeth called, hopping off the fence to follow Mel.

"Why not? My mother is going to New York City to visit some friends next weekend. I'll be here alone except for the housekeeper. All I have to do is sneak out and saddle Mel. It's only two or three miles from here to school, all back roads."

With that part of the plan out of the way, Lindsay thought the rest sounded easy. "Elizabeth, Marissa, and I can tell our parents we have to go back to school to help Ms. Iver decorate Founder's Hall for Founder's Day. We'll meet behind the library at seven o'clock and wait for Aurora to show up."

"Do the buses run that late?" Elizabeth asked.

"I'm not sure," Lindsay answered. Actually, she knew absolutely nothing about the Middleford city buses because she had never ridden one in her life. "Can't you get a ride?"

Elizabeth shook her head. "We only have one car. Besides, my parents will be busy at the restaurant."

Lindsay thought back to the morning the girls had met beside the Randall Hall auditorium in their makeshift uniforms. Now she understood why they had seen Elizabeth walking across the parking lot. Unlike the other kids, whose parents drove them to school each morning, she had to take the bus. "Don't worry about it," Lindsay said. "My mother and I will pick you up at your house."

"No," Elizabeth said quickly, her eyes darting to the ground. "Pick me up at the restaurant."

Marissa had been listening from her perch on the fence. "Look, we can figure out the details later," she said impatiently as Mel approached. "The real question is, what do we do if we get there and discover Chas has already put the pony in the library?"

"That's easy," Aurora said. "We take the pony out and put Mel in."

"But what if Chas shows up with the pony while we're there?" Marissa insisted.

"That's your job," Lindsay replied. "While we put Mel in the library, you watch for Chas. If he shows up, you distract him long enough for us to get out and lock the door."

"How am I supposed to do that?" Marissa asked.

"Oh, you'll think of something," Aurora said, pulling back the reins to bring Mel to a halt in front of Marissa. "Just wrestle him to the ground and put a lip lock on him."

"Oh, shut up," Marissa shot back. "And get that smelly horse out of my face."

Lindsay frowned. Ever since the water fight at the mall, Aurora and Marissa had been acting almost friendly toward each other, and Lindsay wanted to keep it that way—at least until after Founder's Day. "Don't start, you two," she warned.

"Start what?" Aurora asked innocently, sliding off Mel. She offered her hand and Lindsay hopped down, feeling very brave. "Your turn," Aurora continued, handing the reins to Elizabeth. "Marissa would join you, but she's worried she might chip one of her nails."

"I am not," Marissa snapped. "And I'm not scared, either, if that's what you think."

"Then come on," Elizabeth offered. She climbed to the top rung of the fence and hopped onto Mel's back. "We'll take it slow, I promise."

"Sure, why not?" Marissa said coolly. She scrambled to the top of the fence and flung one leg over Mel's back.

Instantly, she lost her balance and pitched sideways. With a shriek, she grabbed at Elizabeth, who let out a cry and threw her arms around the horse's neck. Both girls slid to the side, but managed to hang on. With a gasp and a grunt, Elizabeth righted herself while Marissa dragged herself into a sitting position.

Aurora laughed helplessly and Lindsay stifled a giggle.

"Well, what are we waiting for?" Marissa asked as if nothing unusual had happened. "Are we going to ride this horse or not?"

With a sigh, Elizabeth shook the reins and Mel began to walk. Marissa sat stiffly, bouncing against the horse's back with each step.

"Relax," Aurora called. "Follow Mel's rhythm."

"I'm riding him," Marissa said. "Why doesn't he follow my rhythm?"

Aurora laughed and turned to Lindsay. "I kind of like Marissa this way—just a gallop away from a nervous breakdown. It suits her."

"Come on, knock it off," Lindsay said, hoisting herself onto the fence. "Marissa's okay. Besides, we've got to stick together if we want to pull off this Founder's Day stunt."

"Okay, okay. Listen, now that we're friends again, tell me—what's Will Dalton really like?"

"Boring," Lindsay admitted. "And real set in his ways. More like an old man than a kid."

"So why did you start hanging out with him?"

She shrugged. Looking back on it now, she wasn't really sure. "How's Henry?" she asked.

"Okay. You know, he's a cool guy except for this one totally lame thing. He has a massive crush on Marissa!"

"He told you that?"

"Not in so many words, but he's always asking questions about her. Anyhow, all you have to do is look at him when she walks by. He practically starts drooling."

Aurora snickered and went on talking—something about Evan and an Ultimate Frisbee tournament—but Lindsay wasn't listening. Her chest felt hollow and she didn't know why. What did she care if Henry had the hots for Marissa? *It's not as if I'm interested in him or anything,* she told herself.

"Whoa!" Elizabeth suddenly shrieked. "*Whoooo-aaaa!*"

Lindsay and Aurora looked up just in time to see Mel buck as a squirrel scurried under his feet. Then he took off, heading across the ring at a canter.

"Stop, Mel!" Aurora yelled, wildly waving her arms. "*Stop!*"

But Mel was beyond obeying. As the squirrel disappeared into the grass, he sped up to a full gallop. Elizabeth clung to his mane and pressed her head against his neck. Behind her, Marissa had one arm around Elizabeth and one up in the air like a rodeo rider.

The fence was dead ahead. Marissa let out a squeal as Mel jumped gracefully into the air. He cleared the fence easily and hit the ground running.

"Come on!" Aurora cried, taking off after them.

With her heart pounding, Lindsay followed Aurora across the ring. Together they scrambled over the fence. But by the time they jumped into the grass on the other side, Mel had slowed to a trot. He turned and headed back toward them, his eyes shining and his tail swishing. He looked very pleased with himself as he sauntered up to Aurora.

"Are you all right?" Lindsay asked anxiously, looking up at Elizabeth and Marissa.

"I thought I was going to die!" Elizabeth exclaimed breathlessly. "He just took off! It was as if we were flying!"

"What about you, Marissa?" Aurora asked, reaching up to clutch Mel's reins. "Are you okay?"

Marissa peered around Elizabeth's shoulder. Her eyes were shining like Mel's, and her hair was wild and windblown. "That was incredible!" she breathed. "Can we do it again?" With that, her eyes fluttered closed and she slumped forward in a dead faint.

CHAPTER
TWELVE

*S*o then she fainted," Lindsay told Henry as they left Assembly together on Monday morning.

"Fainted?" Henry gasped. "Marissa?"

"Yep. She fell against Elizabeth with so much force, she knocked Elizabeth off the horse. And Marissa came tumbling after," she added with a grin.

But Henry wasn't smiling. "Was Marissa—I mean, were either of them hurt?"

"Elizabeth got a few bruises, that's all. Marissa landed on Elizabeth and didn't even come to. Aurora had to get one of those little smelling salts capsules out of the first aid kit in the barn and break it under her nose."

"Wow, it must have been so scary when Mel took off," Henry said. "Marissa was really brave."

Lindsay rolled her eyes. "If she's so brave, how come she stayed home today but Elizabeth is here?"

"Everyone deals with trauma in a different way," Henry said. "Marissa is a very sensitive person." He pointed across the quad. "There's Will Dalton. I guess you want to go walk with him."

Before Lindsay could answer, Will spotted her and jogged over. "Hey, Linds," he said, reaching for her books.

"Don't," she said, pulling away.

"Huh? Why not?"

"Well, um . . . I'm walking with Henry this morning."

"Hi there," Henry said, smiling weakly. He looked a little nervous, probably because Will Dalton was approximately twice his size.

Will shot Lindsay a puzzled look. "I guess I'll see you at lunch then."

It would be easy to lie and say she had a doctor's appointment at lunchtime. But Lindsay knew she had to follow her heart. And that meant telling Will the truth. "Uh . . . well," she began, "I'm going to sit with the girls today."

Will scowled. "Lindsay, what's with you? I know we lost the football game on Saturday, but that's no reason to get down on me. If Connor Smythe had caught that last pass—"

"Will, there's a UAU meeting after school today. And I'm going."

"What?" he cried. "What are you, some kind of weirdo?"

Lindsay smiled. "Yeah. Yeah, I guess I am."

Will looked completely baffled. "Well," he said uncertainly, "I guess I'll see you around then."

Lindsay nodded. "I guess I'll see you, too."

Will just stood there. "Weird," he muttered, shaking his head. Then slowly he turned and walked away.

"Wow, that was too cool!" Henry exclaimed as soon as Will was out of earshot. "Are you really going to the UAU meeting this afternoon?"

"Sure. We have to write that letter to the trustees if we ever want to get the uniform rule changed, don't we?"

Grinning, Henry reached into his jacket pocket and pulled out a fat yellow pencil. He tapped it twice against his leg, cried, *"Voilà!"*—and suddenly the pencil turned into a giant bouquet of flowers. "Welcome back, Lindsay," he said, handing them to her.

Lindsay's heart did a joyous tap dance against her rib cage. The flowers were only faded crepe paper, but to her they were the most beautiful objects in the entire world. Suddenly, Henry's mad passion for Marissa seemed totally meaningless. *What's a schoolboy crush compared to a mature relationship like ours?* she asked herself.

Lindsay laid the crepe paper bouquet on top of her books, clutched them to her chest, and started walking. She wished she had something special to give to Henry, but what? And then she thought about the girls' plan to put a stallion in the library on Founder's Day and outdo Chas Randall. What would delight Henry more than to hear about that?

"Henry," she said, turning to him, "do you want to know a secret?"

"Where the heck is she?" Lindsay asked, staring into the twilight. It was Friday night, and she was huddled

126

behind an oak tree at the back of the Randall Hall library with Marissa and Elizabeth.

For the third time in the last five minutes, Marissa tiptoed to the library and peered through one of the back windows. "It's seven-fourteen," she announced in a loud whisper.

Lindsay sighed and kicked the oak tree in frustration. The lights in the library were on, the wastebaskets were empty, and the door was unlocked, which meant the janitors had finished with their cleaning and had moved on to other buildings. In other words, it was the perfect moment to put Mel in the library. Only one problem— Aurora hadn't shown up yet.

"It's so cold," Elizabeth said through chattering teeth. "Look, I can see my breath."

Lindsay crossed her arms and slipped her fingers under her armpits. Indian summer was over and the weather had turned chilly.

"Seven-fifteen," Marissa announced.

"All right already." Lindsay groaned. There was nothing to do but wait and hope that Aurora hadn't been caught by the housekeeper, gotten lost, or worse. Lindsay sat down with her back against the trunk of the tree and tried to think of something else.

It was hard to believe that Founder's Day was tomorrow. The week had flashed by like a video stuck on fast forward. Lindsay had spent all her spare time working with the UAU committee: composing a letter to the trustees, collecting signatures for a student petition, and begging teachers to write their own antiuniform letters to the board.

Lindsay smiled, remembering the look on Ms. Iver's

face when she had walked into the Monday afternoon UAU meeting with Aurora, Henry, and Evan. Her teacher's green eyes had sparkled as she'd said, "How's that round-peg-in-a-square-hole problem working out?"

"I think I found my round hole to fit into," Lindsay had replied. "I'll let you know on Founder's Day."

A cold wind rustled the grass, bringing Lindsay back to the present. She took off her glasses and sucked on one of the earpieces, trying to think. At least Chas hadn't shown up—not yet, anyway.

"Hey, I think I hear something," Marissa hissed. "Listen!"

There was a faint noise coming from the quad. It didn't sound like horse's hooves, though. As Lindsay listened, it grew louder. It was sort of a whirring sound, like a fan or . . .

"A bicycle!" Elizabeth whispered. "It sounds like a bike."

"Darn it!" a voice exclaimed. It was Aurora. "Ouch!"

"Over here!" Lindsay called.

There was a thud and a low curse. And then another sound became audible—a sort of clucking. Lindsay shot Marissa and Elizabeth a quizzical look. They shrugged, as baffled as she was.

Suddenly, Aurora appeared around the corner of the library, riding an old-fashioned red bicycle with fat tires and handlebar streamers. The light from the library windows illuminated her grimacing face.

"Where's Mel?" Marissa demanded, hurrying out of the shadows.

"He stepped in a woodchuck hole this afternoon while

my mother was riding him," Aurora panted, still pedaling toward them. "His left front leg is sprained. The vet said we can't ride him for at least a month."

"Oh no!" Elizabeth moaned. "What are we going to do now?"

The bicycle wobbled to a halt. "I came as fast as I could," Aurora said, wiping her sweating brow. "This bike is a relic. My mother bought it at an antique auction. She's said it's the kind she used to ride when she was a kid—about a hundred years ago, I guess."

"What's that?" Marissa suddenly cried, pointing to the back of the bike.

Aurora shrugged apologetically. "I brought the only animal I could carry," she explained. "I figured it was better than nothing."

Lindsay stepped closer. The bike had a carrier rack behind the seat. A wire cage was tied to the rack with bungie cords. Inside the cage was a chicken.

"A chicken?" Lindsay shrieked. "You brought a chicken?"

"That's all I could carry," Aurora said.

"Aurora, you flake, it's the Randall Hall Stallions, not the Randall Hall Poultry!" Marissa wailed.

"Look, I told you," Aurora said, her voice rising. "Mel sprained his ankle. What did you want me to do, carry him here?"

"At least you could have brought the pig," Elizabeth said glumly.

"Give me a break!" Aurora practically shouted. "That pig must weigh two hundred pounds. I can barely pedal this stupid bike as it is."

"Keep your voice down," Marissa hissed. She turned to Lindsay. "Okay, Ms. President, what do you suggest we do now?"

Lindsay groaned. Her beautiful plan was crumbling to dust before her eyes. "I don't know," she admitted. "I guess we put the chicken in the library. I mean, it's better than nothing, right?"

"But what's the point?" Elizabeth asked. "I mean, the pig was because of Mr. Piggle. The stallion was for the Randall Hall Stallions. But what does a chicken have to do with anything?"

"It shows we're not afraid to break with tradition," Aurora proclaimed. "Get it? We're not chicken."

"That's stupid," Marissa said flatly.

"Oh, really," Aurora shot back. "And do you have a better idea, Bubble Brain?"

"Don't call me Bubble Brain, you bran flake," Marissa shouted.

"Shut up, you two!" Lindsay ordered. "Let's just put the chicken in the library and get out of here before someone catches us."

"Right," Aurora agreed. She jumped off her bike and unfastened the latch on the chicken's cage.

"You're going to let it out?" Marissa asked, backing away.

"Why not? She's as tame as a kitten." Aurora produced a small ball of string from her pocket. "We can tie her to the table, just like we were going to do with Mel."

"I brought a huge sheet of plastic," Elizabeth said, pointing to her backpack. "My parents covered the floor with it when they painted the restaurant."

"Good," Lindsay said. "Let's go."

Aurora reached into the cage and grabbed the chicken. The creature let out a squawk, but Aurora held it tightly in her arms. Dropping the bike onto the grass, she started walking toward the front of the library. Elizabeth and Marissa followed.

Lindsay brought up the rear. She was just starting up the library stairs when she heard a rustling in the bushes next to the statue of Charles Bennington Randall. She stopped and spun around. "Who's there?" she whispered.

A small figure dressed in black stepped from behind a bush. He wore a black fedora, and in the gathering dusk, he looked like something out of a 1940s mystery novel. Then he took off his hat and gazed up at her.

"Henry!" Lindsay cried.

The other girls stopped and turned. Henry put his hat back on and ran to join them. "I've got big news," he said breathlessly. Suddenly he stopped and stared at the chicken in Aurora's arms. "What's that?"

"It's a long story," Lindsay said. "What did you come to tell us?"

"I was in Pizza Pete's—you know, the pizza parlor over on Stony Brook Avenue—eating dinner with my parents," he said, talking fast. "Chas was there, too, along with three or four of his friends. I overheard them talking. All that stuff he told Marissa about putting a horse in the library was a trick!"

"A trick?" Marissa repeated. "What do you mean?"

"He never intended to put a pony in the library," Henry explained. "He only said that because he knew you girls would try to outdo him."

"We almost did, too," Marissa said, glaring at Aurora.

"Chas found out from someone about your plan to put Mel in the library," Henry went on urgently. "He said he was going to wait until you girls left, and then take the horse and lead it through the flower bed in front of the office."

"You mean Mr. Bertozzi's prize flowers?" Lindsay asked. "The ones Chas threw your Social Studies book into?"

"You got it," Henry said with a nod. "He said he's going to let the horse trample the flowers. Then he'll tie it up outside with a sign that says RANDY'S RAIDERS STRIKE AGAIN! He figures that when Mr. Bertozzi sees it tomorrow, he'll blow up and suspend you—or maybe even expel you."

"That means Chas must be on his way over here," Elizabeth said, staring uneasily into the gathering darkness.

Henry nodded. "I overheard him say that after he walks Mel through the flower bed, he's going to put a pig in the library. He said you were really dumb to think he'd put a pony in there, because he would never break with Randall Hall tradition."

"Darn!" Lindsay muttered furiously. "I should have known that!"

"That little weasel!" Aurora exclaimed. "I'd like to put a pig in his underwear!"

"What do we do now?" Marissa asked hopelessly.

"I say we hide in the library and wait for Chas to show up with his precious pig," Aurora said. "After he leaves, we can let the pig loose in the flower bed and put up a sign that says CHAS WAS HERE." She smiled wickedly. "Then we'll see who gets suspended!"

Lindsay thought it over. The idea of giving Chas a taste of his own medicine was a tempting one. But to make it happen, she'd have to do the very things she hated Chas for doing: destroying school property, lying, and letting someone else take the blame for her actions. "No," she said at last. "I won't do it."

"You mean you're giving up?" Henry asked in disbelief.

"I didn't say that," Lindsay said with a sly smile. "I propose we hide in the library and wait for Chas to show up with the pig. When he leaves, we take the pig to Aurora's house and leave our chicken in its place. Then tomorrow we tell Chas we've kidnapped—or should I say pignapped—his pig, and if he wants it back, he's got to do all our homework for the next month plus promise he'll never try to trick us again."

"Lindsay," Henry said with awe in his voice, "you are an absolute genius."

Lindsay's insides felt warm and glowing, as if the White House Christmas tree had just been lit in her heart. "Thanks!" she said.

"Enough with the small talk," Aurora broke in. "Chas could show up at any minute. Let's go inside and find a good place to hide."

At that very moment, footsteps resounded through the darkness. Henry and the girls turned to one another, their eyes wide.

"Someone's coming!" Aurora whispered.

"It must be Chas," Henry said.

"What now?" Elizabeth asked.

"Run!" Marissa cried.

*H*enry and the girls ran up the library steps and burst through the doors. "The bathroom!" Lindsay cried, pointing to the tiny lavatory where she had hidden after her pants ripped.

"You girls go on," Henry said.

Lindsay turned to him. "Aren't you coming?"

"Leave this to me," he said with a mysterious smile. "I've got a secret weapon."

There was no time to argue. Lindsay sprinted toward the bathroom with Marissa and Elizabeth right behind her. Aurora brought up the rear, still holding the chicken. The animal had picked up the feeling of panic in the air and had begun to cluck with alarm.

"Hush!" Aurora ordered. The chicken responded with a loud squawk.

With her heart jackhammering against her chest,

Lindsay threw open the door and ran into the unlit bathroom. As she turned to feel for the light switch, her knee slammed into something soft and fleshy. A loud, inhuman grunt came from somewhere near the floor. Lindsay's heart leaped into her throat. She shrieked and fell backward.

After that, everything seemed to happen at once. Lindsay crashed into Marissa, who was directly behind her. Marissa cried, "Hey!" and held up her hands, accidentally shoving Lindsay between the shoulder blades.

"What's happening?" Elizabeth asked anxiously.

"Hey, let me in," Aurora said at the same time.

The bathroom door slammed shut, plunging the room into total darkness. Lindsay fell forward and hit something pointy and hard.

"Ouch!" she wailed.

"Watch out!" an unknown voice cried.

The chicken began to squawk frantically and flap its wings. "Stop it!" Aurora shouted. "Hey, come back here!"

Behind her, Lindsay heard Marissa let out a hysterical scream. Elizabeth gasped. Lindsay felt something feathery brush her face. She ducked and put her arms over her head. One elbow bashed against something hard—the sink?—and the other pressed into something soft.

There was a frightened squeal from floor level. A rough, lumpy thing wiggled between Lindsay's legs, knocking her off balance. "Whaah!" she cried as she fell to the floor.

Lindsay landed on a pair of feet. As she tried to roll

off them, she felt something peck her neck. She threw out her arms wildly and hit feathers. The chicken squawked. A voice cried, "Yow!" Then someone—or something—fell on her, pinning her right arm beneath her back and her left leg beneath her rear end.

"Get off me!" she shouted. "Get—"

The bathroom light blazed on. Lindsay blinked, half blinded. Slowly, her eyes adjusted and she realized she was staring into the face of the person who had fallen on her.

"Chas!"

"Lindsay!"

"Get off me!"

"Believe me, I'm trying."

Chas untangled his fingers from Lindsay's hair and his right foot from the pipe underneath the sink. As he rolled off her, Lindsay scrambled to her knees and looked around the tiny bathroom in disbelief. Aurora, Marissa, and Elizabeth were lying in a jumble on the floor. Aurora's hands and arms were covered with scratches. The chicken was sitting in the sink, clucking unhappily. A fat, pink pig was cowering behind the toilet, uneasily eying the human beings.

But probably the most shocking sight of all was the boy who was kneeling beside the bathroom door, his hair disheveled, his shirt ripped, and his hand on the light switch.

"Fraser!" Lindsay cried. "What are you doing here?"

"Nothing," he said, getting to his feet. "I'm just, you know, helping out."

The girls stared. Aurora untangled herself from Marissa and Elizabeth and sat up. "Now we know how Chas found out about our plan to put Mel in the library," she said accusingly.

"But I thought Mel was a horse," Chas said. "What's with the chicken?"

"Mel sprained his leg," Marissa began. "So Aurora brought the only—"

But Lindsay wasn't interested in talking about farm animals. "*You* told Chas about our plan to put a stallion in the library?" she interrupted, gazing at her brother in astonishment. "But how did you know?"

Fraser shrugged and studied the tile floor. "I did a little detective work, that's all. I eavesdropped on you when you were talking to the girls on the phone. Then I overheard you calling Elizabeth this afternoon. You said you'd pick her up at quarter to seven. So I called Chas."

"You double-crossed me!" Lindsay cried angrily, jumping to her feet. "I asked for your help and you tricked me."

"Don't get hysterical," Fraser said. "I mean, what's the big deal? It's just a joke."

"A joke?" Aurora broke in. "You think trampling Mr. Bertozzi's flowers and blaming it on us is funny? You call trying to get us expelled from Randall Hall a joke?"

"Wait a minute," Fraser said, turning to Chas. "You didn't tell me anything like that. You said you were going to tie up Aurora's horse behind the library and put the pig inside instead."

"Don't listen to them," Chas said. "They don't know what they're talking about."

"We do, too," Elizabeth insisted. "Henry overheard Chas bragging to his friends in Pizza Pete's. He wants to get us in trouble so Mr. Bertozzi will kick us out of school."

Fraser looked stunned. He glanced from Chas to Lindsay and back again. Nobody spoke. Then suddenly there was a sharp bang from somewhere outside the library. The chicken squawked. The pig squealed and squeezed farther behind the toilet.

"What was that?" Marissa asked anxiously.

"It sounded like a firecracker," Elizabeth said.

There was a small window with frosted glass above the toilet. Chas climbed onto the toilet seat and tried to open the window, but it wouldn't budge. "I think it's painted shut," he said.

Bang! Bang!

"What if something happened to Henry?" Elizabeth whispered, wide-eyed.

"Henry's out there?" Chas asked.

"I think he stayed behind to distract you while we brought the chicken inside," Marissa said.

"But I'm not out there," Chas answered. "I'm right here."

"We know that now," Aurora said impatiently. "Come on. Let's go into the library and sneak a peek out the window."

Marissa opened the bathroom door a crack and peered out. "All clear."

Aurora, Marissa, Elizabeth, and Chas tiptoed out of the bathroom. Fraser started after them, but Lindsay grabbed his arm and held him back.

"Don't you want to make sure Henry's all right?" Fraser asked.

But Lindsay had a pretty good idea of what Henry was up to. "Henry can take care of himself," she said. "I want to talk to you."

"Oh, all right," Fraser muttered, thrusting his hands into his jeans pockets. "Talk."

Lindsay closed the bathroom door and gazed at her brother. She could feel tears welling up inside her, and they made her furious. Everyone else in her family knew how to keep their cool in emotional situations. No matter how upsetting things got, they remained reasonable and logical. *Well, I can be reasonable, too,* she told herself. She gritted her teeth and forced back the tears. "Why did you trick me, Fraser?" she asked.

Fraser's cheeks flushed pink. He looked angry and embarrassed and confused, all at the same time. "I didn't know Chas was planning to get you in trouble. All he told me was that you girls wanted to put a horse in the library. He asked me to help him uphold the *real* Randy Hall tradition."

"Is that all that matters to you—Randall Hall tradition?" Lindsay demanded. "What about me?"

"Hey, I tried to warn you," he said defensively. "Remember when you talked to me in the basement last week? I told you to leave the pig stunt to the sixth-grade boys."

"But why? Why can't girls be part of Randall Hall, too?"

"Girls can," Fraser said, throwing up his arms in frustration. "But why does the girl in the lead—the one who causes all the fuss and grabs all the attention—always have to be *you?*"

Lindsay opened her mouth to speak, and the dam she had built inside her burst open. "I hate Randall Hall," she sobbed. "Just because I'm your little sister, everyone expects me to be talented and charming and never stick my foot in my mouth. But I'm not like you, Fraser. When I feel something, I just have to blurt it out."

"That's exactly my point!" Fraser exclaimed. "Ever since the first day of school, everyone has been talking about you. 'Did you hear what Lindsay said? Did you see what Lindsay did?' Nobody pays any attention to me anymore. I'm just Lindsay Tavish's boring big brother, that's all."

Lindsay paused, puzzled. "What are you talking about?" she asked, wiping a tear from her eye. "You're a big tennis champion. I don't do anything special."

"Are you kidding? You took this school by storm. I mean, take the uniform rule. The kids have been complaining about having to wear uniforms for years, but no one did anything about it until you showed up. And what about the way you handled Chas Randall? He waltzed into Assembly the first day, ready to take over. But you put him in his place."

"But I didn't plan those things," Lindsay insisted. "I don't have to practice and train to win tennis matches like you do. Ideas just pop into my brain and I act on them. Sometimes they work out and sometimes—"

"—you make a total fool of yourself and embarrass me half to death," Fraser finished. "But that's what makes you so amazing, Linds. You speak your mind. You take chances." He looked her in the eye. "You know, I think you really will be the first woman president someday."

Lindsay was speechless. All this time she'd assumed Fraser thought she was nothing but an embarrassing pain in the neck. *Now it turns out he admires me almost as much as I admire him,* she thought with amazement. *In fact, it almost sounds as if he's a little jealous of me.*

But that concept was too much for Lindsay to get her brain around. She felt almost relieved when Fraser wedged her head in the crook of his arm and gave her a scalp-pounding noogie. "Stop it!" she squealed, giggling and squirming. The hen and pig joined in, clucking and grunting.

"Hey, get out here, you two," Aurora called from the library. "Henry's setting off some kind of bomb!"

Lindsay and Fraser ran into the library and joined the others at the window. Outside the library, two shadowy figures in orange coveralls were crouching behind the statue of Charles Bennington Randall. Henry was nearby, hiding behind a tree. Every few seconds there was a loud *crack,* and a puff of smoke appeared at his feet.

"I knew it!" Lindsay exclaimed. "Henry's throwing magic fireballs to scare off the janitors. He makes them himself. You toss them against something hard and *pow!*"

"This is our chance to get out of here," Marissa said. "Does this place have a back door?"

"We can't leave without Henry," Elizabeth protested.

"Why not?" Chas asked. "Come on, Fraser, let's tie the pig to the table and leave a sign so everyone knows who did it."

"You're going to take all the credit for yourself?" Aurora broke in. "What about us?"

"What do you mean, what about you? Fraser and I brought the pig. All you brought is a stupid chicken."

"Because you tricked us," Lindsay said.

"It worked, too, didn't it?" Chas said smugly.

"Chas," Fraser asked, "did anyone ever tell you you're an arrogant little twerp?"

Chas looked as if he'd been slapped in the face. Then he recovered and said, "Don't tell me you've switched sides! What happened—did your baby sister threaten to tattle on you to Mommy and Daddy?"

Fraser lunged forward as if he was about to slam one of his famous backstrokes. Instead, he grabbed Chas by the front of his shirt and lifted him into the air. "I was never on your side," he said. "Not the way you thought, anyway. And if you ever try to trick my sister again, I'll use your nose for a tennis ball."

At that moment, the library door flew open and Henry ran in. His face was flushed and his hair was windblown. Fraser released Chas. Everyone turned toward Henry.

"What's going on?" he asked, looking around uncertainly. "Chas, Fraser, what are you doing here?"

"Never mind that," Lindsay said. "What's happening outside?"

"The janitors showed up, so I tossed some fireballs at them," Henry said. "I meant to scare them away long enough for us to escape, but I think my plan worked a little too well. I heard one of them say 'He's got a gun.' Then the other guy said, 'I'm calling the cops,' and they ran off."

"The police?" Marissa gasped. "Oh no!"

"What are we waiting for?" Elizabeth said. "Let's get out of here."

"But what about the animals?" Aurora asked. "Do we leave the pig, the chicken, or neither?"

"The pig," Chas said firmly.

"The chicken," Aurora, Marissa, and Elizabeth said together.

"Why don't we leave both?" Fraser suggested.

"Are you crazy?" Chas demanded. "Everyone will understand what the pig is doing here, but what about the chicken? I mean, what does a chicken have to do with Randall Hall tradition?"

Lindsay thought it over. Then all at once it hit her—an absolutely brilliant solution. "I've got it!" she cried.

She ran to the circulation desk and found a piece of poster paper and a Magic Marker. Quickly she wrote: LONG LIVE RANDALL HALL—A SCHOOL WHERE UPPITY CHICKS AND MALE CHAUVINIST PIGS HAVE LEARNED TO LIVE SIDE BY SIDE! Then she held up the sign for everyone to read.

"Oh, corny!" Fraser groaned.

"But clever," Henry said. "I say we go for it."

"No way!" Chas cried. "I'm the one who brought the pig. I'm not sharing the glory with a bunch of girls."

"Face it, Chas," Aurora said. "You have no choice—unless you want us to tell Mr. Bertozzi what you planned to do to his precious flowers."

Lindsay propped the sign against one of the tables. "Truce?" she asked, holding out her hand.

Chas scowled, and then reluctantly shook it. "Truce," he muttered. "For tonight, anyway."

"*Dios mío,*" Elizabeth cried suddenly. "Look!"

Lindsay spun around and her mouth fell open. The

pig and the chicken had escaped from the bathroom when no one was looking. Now the chicken was sitting on the circulation desk, happily pecking at a stack of overdue notices. The pig was in the corner, rooting through a pile of books it had knocked off a nearby bookshelf.

"Oh no," Fraser moaned. "We must have left the bathroom door open."

"Well, don't just stand there," Aurora said. "Let's get them."

Lindsay and the girls surrounded the chicken. "Come here, pretty girl," Aurora said, reaching for it. The hen responded by rearing back and pecking Aurora's arm. "Ow!" she wailed, pulling away. The chicken flapped over her head and landed on a book cart.

"Now you've scared her," Marissa said accusingly.

"I've scared *her*?" Aurora cried, holding her arm. "What about *me*? That chicken is dangerous."

"Here, chick, chick, chick," Lindsay cooed. Gingerly, she reached for the chicken. It let out a piercing squawk and flew over her head, releasing bird droppings on the carpet as it went.

"*Ew*! It made a mess!" Marissa cried.

"Watch out!" Henry yelled from behind her.

Marissa turned as the pig ran between her legs. She gasped and fell backward. The pig squealed and veered to the left. Chas, Fraser, Henry, Lindsay, Aurora, and Elizabeth took off after it. The pig ran under the tables and between the shelves, knocking over chairs and books as it went.

"I never knew a pig could run so fast!" Fraser panted.

The pig zigzagged between a row of overturned chairs and collided with the chicken. The startled hen let out a squawk and flew at Chas.

"Get away from me, you birdbrain!" he shouted, ducking as the chicken flapped over his head and landed on the card catalog.

Elizabeth grabbed for the bird, but it hopped to the floor, leaving her with a handful of feathers.

"There he goes!" Lindsay cried, pointing as the pig shot out from under a table.

Chas flung himself at the animal like a defensive lineman sacking a quarterback, but the pig wiggled away and Chas was left in a puddle of pig drool. "Yuck!" he wailed. "I've been slimed!"

"Uh-oh," Henry said, stopping short at one of the windows. "Look." A police car, its red light flashing, was cruising slowly across the quad.

"Let's go!" Elizabeth cried.

"But what about the mess?" Fraser asked. "The place is a total disaster area."

Lindsay looked around and her heart sank. Chairs and books were scattered everywhere. Feathers and chicken droppings covered the tabletops. Up on the magazine rack, the chicken clucked softly, while the pig rooted in the carpet. "We can't leave things like this," she said.

The words were barely out of her mouth when the red light of the police car flashed through the library windows. There were voices outside and the sound of the car doors opening.

"There's no time to clean up," Aurora insisted. "We have to go *now*."

"But how?" Marissa asked. "We can't walk out the front door. They'll see us."

"The back windows," Chas said urgently. "Come on!"

Everyone ran to the back of the library. There was a large window behind the librarian's desk with a philodendron plant on the sill. Fraser vaulted over the desk, removed the plant, and unlocked the window. He pushed hard. With a loud *crack*, it flew open.

Aurora, Marissa, and Elizabeth scrambled out the window, followed by the boys. Lindsay brought up the rear. She climbed onto the windowsill and glanced back at the library. Then suddenly a horrible thought struck her. The sign! She had written it before the pig and chicken got loose and made a mess.

Lindsay shuddered, picturing Mr. Bertozzi walking into the trashed library and reading the line about the "uppity chicks and male chauvinist pigs." There were 214 male chauvinist pig suspects at Randall Hall, but only 4 uppity chicks—and Mr. Bertozzi was going to come looking for them.

I've got to get that sign, Lindsay thought frantically. She began to climb back down from the windowsill—and froze. The library door was opening. She caught a glimpse of a blue uniform. The police! With her heart in her throat, Lindsay leaped out the window and followed her friends into the night.

*F*ounder's Day, here we come," Mr. Tavish said as he pulled into the crowded Randall Hall parking lot. He parked the car and climbed out. Mrs. Tavish and Fraser followed.

"It's a beautiful day for a celebration," Mrs. Tavish remarked. "Warm sun, a cool breeze. And look at those colors!"

Lindsay squinted out of the back window. The trees were a patchwork of red, gold, and orange leaves, but right now she wasn't thinking about fall foliage. Her mind was on the library and the mess that she and her friends had left.

The way she saw it, the whole stupid fiasco was her fault. If she hadn't convinced the girls to outdo Chas by putting a horse in the library, none of this would have happened. *And then there's the sign*, she reminded herself. How clever she had felt when she thought up the line about "uppity chicks and male chauvinist pigs." But it was that very line that was going to tip off Mr. Bertozzi. And soon she was going to be in trouble big time.

With a sigh Lindsay thought back to the day Ms. Iver had told her to "just be yourself." Sure, it had sounded like a good idea at the time. For a while there she had even convinced herself that being bold, passionate, and outspoken was a good thing. So what if she would never be charming and gracious like the rest of her family? She was Lindsay, the leader. Lindsay, the righter of wrongs. Lindsay, the first woman president of the United States.

Lindsay snorted through her nose. *Who am I fooling?* she asked herself. *I'll never be president. I couldn't get elected dog catcher after last night.*

"Are you planning on spending the entire morning in the car?" Mr. Tavish asked, peering through the rear window at her.

Lindsay managed a weak laugh. She got out and gazed up at the blue and white bunting that was strung above the doors of the auditorium. WELCOME STUDENTS AND PARENTS, it said.

"I wonder how welcome *we're* going to be," Fraser muttered as he and Lindsay followed their parents across the parking lot.

It was the first thing he had said to her since they left the library last night. *He blames me for what happened,* she thought. *And why not?* But she was going to make it up to him, and to everyone else, as well. When Mr. Bertozzi confronted her, she was going to say she had put the pig and the chicken in the library all by herself. Maybe she would be suspended, or even expelled. But she didn't care. She deserved it.

"Don't worry, Fraser," she began. "I've got everything figured out. I—"

But Fraser had spotted Mason Fitzpatrick arriving with his parents. "Mom, Dad, I'm going to talk to Mason," he called. He waved to Lindsay as he hurried away.

Lindsay and her parents walked into the quad. All the buildings were decorated with festive blue and white bunting. Rows of folding chairs faced the statue of Charles Bennington Randall. In front of the statue, a platform had been erected with a podium and a several folding chairs. Mr. Bertozzi was standing behind the platform, chatting with a group of four men and two women. *Probably the trustees,* Lindsay thought, her stomach tightening.

"How's this?" Mr. Tavish asked, taking a seat about halfway back. Lindsay nodded and sat down beside her mother.

"Isn't it exciting being a member of the first coed class, Lindsay?" Mrs. Tavish asked.

"It's a real honor," Mr. Tavish said.

"I'll admit I was a little worried about you, honey," Mrs. Tavish went on. "It's not easy coming into a pressure cooker situation like this, and—let's face it—you're not famous for your diplomacy."

"But you proved you could handle it," Mr. Tavish said.

Mrs. Tavish chuckled. "I guess we Tavishes are just destined to be pioneers."

Lindsay slumped in her chair. She felt like such an impostor. Her parents thought she was upholding the family tradition of grace under pressure. Instead she had masterminded the biggest disaster of her entire life.

Forcing back tears, she turned from her parents and looked around the quad. She spotted Mr. and Mrs. Lopez standing outside the auditorium, talking enthusiastically to Mr. Brack while Elizabeth looked on in embarrassment. Marissa and her father were admiring Mr. Bertozzi's prize flower bed. Aurora was sitting with her mother in the back row, nervously twisting her hair and bouncing in her seat.

Lindsay was about to search for Chas and Henry when a quavering voice said, "Good morning, everyone!" She looked up to see a very old man with gray hair and a mustache standing at the podium. He tapped the microphone a few times and cleared his throat.

"I am Horace Randall, the oldest living alumnus of Randall Hall," he announced, "and I am delighted to welcome you to Founder's Day. Please take your seats, ladies and gentlemen. The festivities are about to begin."

The students and their parents hurried to sit down. Horace Randall went on to tell everyone that Charles Bennington Randall was his uncle. He said a lot of other things, as well, but Lindsay was too busy watching Mr. Bertozzi to pay much attention. The headmaster was sitting on the platform with the trustees. He was squinting grimly, and Lindsay couldn't help imagining that he was thinking about how pleasant it was going to be to expel the girls and restore Randall Hall to its former glory as an all-boys' school.

"And now," Horace Randall said, "I am pleased to introduce Randall Hall's headmaster, George Bertozzi."

Lindsay's stomach knotted. Fraser slipped into the empty seat beside her and stared down at his shoes. Lindsay wished she could tell him not to worry, but this wasn't the time.

"As you know," Mr. Bertozzi said in his booming baritone, "Randall Hall has a number of unique traditions. One of them began in 1910 when a group of sixth graders sneaked a pig into the library on Founder's Day in honor of their headmaster, Mr. Bartholomew Piggle."

The audience chuckled appreciatively. Lindsay swallowed hard and squirmed in her seat.

"As you may also know," he continued, "Randall Hall went coed this year."

There was a bit of scattered applause and some whispering, but unlike the first day of school, no one booed.

"I, like many at Randall Hall, was against the idea of bringing girls onto the campus," Mr. Bertozzi said. He smiled thinly, and Lindsay was certain he was looking right at her. She stared down at her hands and coughed nervously.

"Boys and girls, mothers and fathers," Mr. Bertozzi proclaimed, "at this time I'd like you all to join me in the library. I think you'll be very interested in what you find."

A buzz of curiosity passed through the crowd. Mr. Bertozzi left the platform and headed toward the library entrance. Alumni wearing blue-and-white arm bands took up positions at the end of each row and ushered everyone single file toward the library.

Lindsay followed her parents. She felt stunned, almost numb. She just couldn't believe Mr. Bertozzi could be so mean. Sure, he had always come across as a stern, humorless sort of person. But to display the chaos in the library to the entire student body and their parents, maybe even to expel the girls in front of everybody—that was downright cruel.

The library door was only a few yards away. Lindsay knew it was now or never. She had to tell Mr. Bertozzi the whole stunt had been her idea. She had to save her friends. But first she had to tell her parents the truth. She wasn't a pioneer. She was a complete and total failure.

"Mom, Dad," she began, gathering up all her courage, "before we go inside, I have something to tell you . . ."

She paused. Was that laughter coming from inside the library? It was! Then a woman's voice exclaimed, "How clever!"

"What were you going to say, Lindsay?" her father asked.

"Uh . . . uh . . ." At that moment the line moved forward. A tidal wave rolled through Lindsay's stomach, and her knees felt as if they were made of Slinkys. She stepped into the crowded library—and stopped dead in her tracks.

All the mess—the overturned chairs, the scattered books, the chicken droppings and pig drool—had been cleaned up. A sheet of plastic had been spread out neatly on the carpet beneath one of the tables. The pig sat on one side of the table, tied to the leg with a leash, happily lapping up a bowl of milk. The chicken lay on the opposite end, peacefully clucking. Lindsay's sign was propped up between them.

Mr. and Mrs. Tavish read the sign and burst out

laughing. "Lindsay, did you have something to do with this?" her mother asked.

"Well," she said, "sort of."

"It's wonderful!" her father exclaimed.

"It is?" she asked in disbelief.

"The sign was Lindsay's idea," Fraser said. "Pretty clever, huh?"

Lindsay gazed at him in astonishment. Could it be he wasn't mad at her after all?

Mrs. Tavish smiled. "A dollop of tradition, a dollop of humor—and a serious message underneath. It's perfect."

"It's a very clever concept," Mr. Tavish agreed. "It shows a great deal of creativity and, dare I say it, diplomacy."

"But I didn't do any of it the way you would have wanted me to," Lindsay protested. "I mean, I wasn't charming or gracious or any of that stuff. I only got involved to show up Chas Randall because he's such a pompous pain in the neck. And then everything went wrong." Lindsay knew she was babbling, but she couldn't stop herself. "The chicken was supposed to be a horse, only he sprained his leg; and then the pig and the chicken got loose, and the police came, and—"

"But the really impressive part was how Lindsay brought the girls and Chas Randall together to pull off the stunt," Fraser broke in. "He's totally against having girls at Randall Hall, but Lindsay convinced him to put aside his differences for a common cause."

Lindsay could hardly believe her ears. "You mean, for once I didn't embarrass you?" she asked.

Fraser shook his head. "I thought we worked this out

last night. I was wrong to put you down for just being yourself." He shrugged. "Anyhow, maybe being a calm, cool, and collected Tavish isn't all it's cracked up to be. I mean, last night was kind of fun—in a wild, weird, *Lindsay* kind of way."

"You may not do things exactly like the rest of the family, Lindsay," Mr. Tavish said, "but the bottom line is, what you did worked."

Mrs. Tavish nodded. "I'm very proud of you, sweetheart," she said, kissing Lindsay's cheek.

Tears of happiness filled Lindsay's eyes. Her parents approved! And the amazing thing was, she hadn't had to change herself to make it happen. She'd managed to please her parents—*and* Fraser—just by being herself.

By now everyone had managed to squeeze into the library. Mr. Bertozzi clapped his hands for silence. "It's true I was against admitting girls to Randall Hall," he said. "But the four girls who have entered the sixth grade this year have proved to me they have much to contribute to our school." He smiled. "Oh, I can't say it has all been smooth sailing. But as this clever stunt points out, we've learned to settle our differences with humor and understanding."

The crowd broke into applause. Lindsay beamed.

"Ladies and gentlemen," Mr. Bertozzi said, "please return to your seats. Lindsay, Aurora, Marissa, and Elizabeth," he added sternly, "may I have a word with you?"

With a dark sense of foreboding, Lindsay joined Mr. Bertozzi behind the circulation desk. The other girls followed, their heads hung low. Lindsay's stomach tightened as Mr. Bertozzi gazed down at them. He wasn't smiling now.

"Mr. Bertozzi," she began, her words tumbling out like rocks in a landslide, "don't blame the others. It was all my fault. I wasn't watching the animals and they got loose and—"

"No way," Aurora interrupted. "The chicken was mine. I should have had it under control."

"What about me?" Elizabeth said. "If I'd remembered to put down the plastic sheet, the chicken wouldn't have messed on the carpet."

"Actually," Marissa admitted, "if I hadn't repeated something Chas Randall told me at the mall last week, none of this would have happened in the first place."

"Yeah, but—" Lindsay began.

"Enough!" Mr. Bertozzi bellowed. "Frankly, I don't want to know what happened here last night." He sighed and ran his hand over his face. "Girls, the point you were trying to get across was an excellent one. But your method left a bit to be desired."

"I'm sorry, sir," Lindsay said sheepishly. "I guess we got a little carried away."

"To say the least. Imagine my surprise when the police called me last night to say the library had been vandalized. When I walked in here this morning, I was ready to expel all four of you girls. But Ms. Iver calmed me down and convinced me your hearts were in the right place. She and I cleaned up the mess together."

"Wow, thanks," Aurora said with feeling.

Mr. Bertozzi smiled. "You're welcome." The smile vanished. "Now, let's talk punishment. You and your cohorts—I'll leave it up to you, Lindsay, to round up all of them—will stay after school every day for the next month to help the janitors clean the library."

"Yes, sir."

"Furthermore, I want you to check on the animals throughout the day. Give them water and clean up their messes. And when the Founder's Day celebration is over, get them out of here!"

"Yes, sir. Of course, sir."

"Now go before I change my mind!"

Lindsay and the girls hurried outside. Henry was waiting for them. "Can you believe our good luck?" he asked.

"I almost freaked when I walked in there," Aurora exclaimed. "It was as if someone had answered my prayers."

"Someone did, and her name is Ms. Iver," Lindsay said. Quickly she filled Henry in on what Mr. Bertozzi had said.

"One whole month of staying after school? Yuck!" Henry cried.

"It could have been worse," Elizabeth said. "Lots worse."

"We got off easy," Marissa agreed.

"Thanks to Lindsay," Aurora said. "If she hadn't thought up that sign, Mr. Bertozzi would have skinned us alive."

"Hey, look," Henry said, "there's Chas."

Lindsay looked up to see Chas walking out of the library with his parents. Mr. Randall looked like an older version of Chas—the same handsome face and sandy-colored hair, the same smug expression. His mother was pretty in a pinched sort of way.

"Hey, Chas, did you hear the news?" Henry called.

Chas left his parents and sauntered over to join them. "What news? That you've got a brain the size of a gnat?"

"Ha, ha. You're killing me," Henry said, deadpan. "Actually, I was referring to Mr. Bertozzi's announcement that we'll be staying after school every day this month to help the janitors clean the library."

Chas's smug expression disappeared. "What? Me, too?"

Lindsay nodded. "And we've decided that we're going to let you clean the bathroom every night."

"Oh, no way. I refuse!"

"Gosh, I thought you'd be honored," Aurora said. "After all, it's a Randall Hall bathroom. It must be simply *dripping* with tradition."

Henry and the girls burst out laughing, but Chas shook his head. "I don't do menial labor."

"Then I guess you'd rather we told Mr. Bertozzi that you planned to destroy his flowers and blame it on us," Aurora said.

Chas was trapped and he knew it. He glanced at his parents, who were talking to one of the trustees, then at Lindsay, then down at the dirt. "Just don't tell anyone about this," he muttered at last. "Especially my parents."

"I promise," Lindsay said, and she meant it.

"Boys and girls, friends and family," a female voice said over the loudspeaker, "your attention, please."

Lindsay looked up to see Ms. Iver standing at the podium.

"Please take your seats," she said to the crowd.

Slowly the students and their parents returned to their

seats. Chas left to join his parents. Lindsay grabbed a seat in the front row and motioned to Henry and the girls to join her. Henry's friend Evan walked by, and Henry called him over, too.

Ms. Iver smiled at the crowd. "In a few minutes we'll all be heading over to the dining hall for a wonderful Founder's Day buffet prepared by the parents and alumni. Then you're all invited to visit your children's classrooms and meet their teachers." She paused. "But first I have a historic announcement to make."

The audience fell silent. All eyes were on Ms. Iver. Lindsay leaned forward in anticipation.

"Some of you have probably heard of the UAU committee," Ms. Iver continued. "The UAU is an organization formed by some of the students to protest the school's uniform policy. The committee has worked very hard during the last few weeks to convince the trustees that Randall Hall should not require students to wear uniforms."

A murmur went through the crowd. Lindsay and the girls exchanged glances.

"Last night the trustees met to discuss the uniform issue," Ms. Iver said, "and they've asked me to communicate their feelings to you."

Lindsay crossed her fingers behind her back.

"The Board of Trustees feels that uniforms are an important part of the Randall Hall philosophy," Ms. Iver said. "They want all students to dress alike in the hope that they will be judged by their character and accomplishments, not by the amount of money they have or the fashions they select."

Lindsay sighed. She understood what Ms. Iver was saying, but she couldn't help feeling the trustees had forgotten a few things—like how boring it was to wear the same thing every day, and how much fun it was to express your personality through your clothing.

"However," Ms. Iver continued, "the trustees do understand the importance of self-expression and individuality among young people. For that reason, they have decided to make every Friday a free day. On that day—and only on that day—students may wear whatever they wish." She glanced at Mr. Bertozzi, who was standing to the right of the platform with a worried expression on his face. "Within reason, of course," she added.

Lindsay let out a whoop of joy. All around her the students leaped to their feet and cheered mightily.

Lindsay looked up to see Henry standing before her. He grabbed her hands and pulled her out of her seat. "We did it!" he shouted. "We did it!" He threw his arms around her and gave her a hug.

With her heart in her throat, she hugged back. Suddenly, she wasn't thinking about the uniform rule. She was feeling Henry's arms around her and breathing in the sweet smell of his shampoo.

Then Evan, Aurora, Marissa, and Elizabeth joined in, and Lindsay was engulfed in a giant hug. Fraser ran up and shouted, "Way to go, Linds!" She managed to untangle her arm long enough to give him a high five.

The cheering was so loud, Lindsay could barely make out what Ms. Iver said next—something about the school providing appropriate uniforms for the girls. Lindsay ducked under her friends' arms and freed herself from their enthusiastic hugs. She looked up at the podium and managed to catch Ms. Iver's eye. Ms. Iver smiled. Lindsay grinned back and mouthed the words, "Thank you."

Ms. Iver winked and leaned into the microphone. The words she spoke next made Lindsay's heart soar.

"Long live Randall Hall!" she cried. "And long live Randy's Raiders!"